RUTHLESS

ALEXIS ABBOTT

PATHFORGERS PUBLISHING

Get an EXCLUSIVE book, **FREE** just as a thank you for signing up for my newsletter! Plus you'll never miss a new release, cover reveal, or promotion!

http://alexisabbott.com/newsletter

CHAPTER 1

The last person in the world I ever expected to hear from again is my wicked witch of a step-mother.

Yet here I am, sitting in her fancy office's reception area, flipping through a magazine as I keep eyeing the receptionist who promised me for the tenth time that Rebecca will be right with me.

My legs are covered with goosebumps; the summer heat outside is sticky and damp, so I dressed light in a skirt and a tank-top, but now that I'm in her office building, I feel like I'm stuck in an icebox. My nipples press against my bra uncomfortably, and I'm trying not to shiver.

I have to appear strong, Confident. All the things I'm not.

I don't even know why I agreed to meet her.

Curiosity, I guess. My dad always said that'd be

my downfall, that I can't ever let anything go no matter how much I should.

No, I know the real reason. Because she's my link to Dimitri.

My step-brother.

The man who I looked up to most in the world, and who ditched me just as fast as his mother.

He broke my heart, and now Rebecca's opened the wounds again. I tried to ignore her message on my phone, but every time I came close, I thought of Dimitri's dark eyes filled with devilish glee.

I remember that last night we spent together before my life came crumbling down around me.

The magazine in my hands is filled with glossy pages of fashion and people who don't look like themselves. I don't understand that. Why bother hiring a famous celebrity for a photoshoot if they're just going to manipulate the lighting and the makeup to the point she doesn't look like herself?

It's the type of things that bored women pay to do, to live as someone else for a little while. Not celebrities being *paid* to do it.

I roll my eyes and glance up at the receptionist again who gives me a smile tighter than her bun. I feel kind of bad for her, honestly. If Rebecca is a boss like she was a mother? Then she's colder than ice, and crueler than Cruella.

How long have I been waiting?

I glance at my watch, and my lip twitches. She's

kept me here for over fifty minutes after insisting I come. I throw the magazine to the side with a huff and fold my arms beneath my chest. She hasn't changed at all. Not even a little, since she kicked me out with nowhere to go and not a cent to my name.

From a mansion to the street in one night. I know, poor little rich girl, right?

Well I'm not rich anymore, and I don't want pity. For the past two years, I've been building up a life for myself. Something I'm proud of.

Something she can't take from me.

The clicking on the floor of stiletto heels draws me back from my stupor.

"Sarah, darling!" Rebecca exclaims with that mild, Russian accent, as if there were nothing wrong between us.

I glance up at her, and my expression goes sour. She looks even better than I remember. I suppose good plastic surgery isn't so much a luxury of the rich as a necessity, and her blonde hair is pulled back to reveal her sharp cheeks and button nose. She looks younger than her forty-five years by at least a decade, and I'm instantly jealous.

My platinum hair tickles my cheeks, and I lift my thrift-store purse to my shoulder as I move to her, coolly.

Don't let her rattle you, I plead with myself, trying to exude casual calm that I certainly don't feel inside. Inside, I'm terrified. This woman is a viper, and she'll chew me up and spit me out with no more thought than most people give to what they eat for breakfast.

She puts her hand on my shoulder and I can feel her glancing there, noticing the wings between my shoulder blades, the black ink a bit faded over the years. I was only seventeen when I got it, but I don't regret it, and I won't let her make me regret it.

I won't let her control me. I just came as a courtesy to my father. It's what he would've wanted, and regardless of the path he went down when he was alive, I owe it to his memory to try to be a better person.

Her office, though, makes me want to be anything but a better person. It's bigger than the entire building I work out of, which barely makes sense. Who needs a penthouse suite as an office? There's a bar over on the far end, a meeting table and couches and chairs littering the room, but she leads me to her desk and an uncomfortable chair that I have to wonder if it was brought in just for me to sit on.

I take a seat across from her as she smiles at me placidly. It's a strange look to her face, like resentment barely hidden by a veil of civility and good manners.

She simply stares at me in silence and I'm forced to speak.

"You're looking well," I say, my tone flat and displeased.

She calls me all the way to Manhattan to make me squirm? Well I'm not going to squirm. I might not have had an easy time of it the past two years, but I worked hard for everything I have and I won't let her take my pride away.

"Thank you," she says cordially, not returning the compliment as she smiles.

And then, it's like she remembers herself. Remembers the fact that she asked me to meet with her, and that she had something she clearly wanted of me. What that something is, I haven't the foggiest idea, but it seems to wipe the resentment from her expression and she looks nearly desperate.

"Sarah, darling, I won't waste any more of your time than I have to. You remember my son, Dimitri?"

I stare at her as if she's just said the stupidest thing, and honestly, she has. He's been my step-brother for seven years, and I lived with him for four. After my father passed away, he was the only real man I had in my life, and even though he's three years older than me, we were close as siblings.

Until she stole him away from me.

My eye twitches as I nod my head.

"Good, good!" she exclaims, her smile so phony I want to smack it off her face.

"Are you two still in contact?"

Again, another stupid question.

"No. Not since you ensured I'd be getting a dose

of homelessness for my eighteenth birthday," I reply with a sneer, and her eyes narrow at me.

Whatever it is she has me here for, though, must be important. I've seen her lose her cool over much less than that, and I can tell from the way she's tightening her fists that she's pissed at me. But she doesn't say anything, just staring at me with that angry expression.

"Well, good," she says coldly before trying to soften the blow with a smile, "because I have a task for you and it's better if you remain... unattached."

"A task?" I can't help the curiosity eking into my voice. What's she want from me, and what does Dimitri have to do with any of it?

Her smile broadens at my interest and she nods.

"Mmm, yes. I've heard from my sources that you work at Upstream Co. as a... receptionist or some sort?"

What the hell? Has she been stalking me? How does she know where I work? Since she kicked me out, I haven't heard from her or thought of her since. The only reason she was even able to get ahold of me is that I didn't get rid of my old cell phone. It has a voice mail my dad left me and I didn't want to lose that. Surprise, surprise when I found a new call from her, though.

"How did you know that?"

She sweeps off my concerns with a bat of her hand and a venomous smile.

"Oh, don't worry about that."

"Well your *sources* are wrong. I'm a bookkeeper."

She rolls her eyes at that too, though part of me gets the feeling that she knew that and was just testing my reaction.

"Regardless of what it is you do there, I have something more important for you, and something I'm willing to pay for. Lord knows if this wasn't dire you wouldn't be here today," she says with another sneer marring her puffed up lips.

The hair on the back of my neck stands up, and with it I stand to leave.

"I'm not going to sit here and be condescended to when you need a favor. I'm not a little girl anymore, *Rebecca*. And I made it just fine without your handouts this far. I only came to see if you realized that kicking an eighteen year old girl out with no support was a bad idea, but apparently, you're fine with your choices."

"Well of course I am," she says, standing as well and looming over me. "You said it yourself. You've done fine without my handouts. You're intrepid. Determined. And that's why I'm willing to pay you an exorbitant fee just to keep doing what you're doing, except instead of working for Upstream, you'll do it for Marala Corp."

Dimitri's company. She'd bought it out a year before she kicked me out, and gave it to Dimitri as a birthday present. It was all over the news.

"You don't have to reply to me now, but it will put your skills to the test. You'll be able to use your photography, your bookkeeping skills, and in the end, I'm willing to part with half a million dollars for six months of work."

My lips part.

I want to protest, to tell her that she can't intimidate and control me with money, but it's like my mind and my mouth are disconnected. After struggling for so long, it would be so nice to just have a nest egg. To not have to worry where rent is coming from, or how I'm going to pay my grocery bill.

And I'd be lying if I said a little part of me isn't curious about what this has to do with Dimitri. Just the memory of him brings back such scandalous thoughts that I have to push away. It was easier to ignore them when I'd cut them all off. Hell, he doesn't even have a Facebook account — I checked.

"So here's what I need you to do," Rebecca says, taking my silence as agreement, and I don't have time to interrupt her. "I need you to approach Dimitri. Tell him that you've missed him, whatever," she says, brushing off emotional displays as if they are nothing more than an annoyance. "You're curious abbout his work, and would love to help him manage his books. And then you'll look at those books, you'll bring me photocopies of those books, and you will be well compensated."

She makes it sound so easy, but I know there's

something she's not telling me. A lot of somethings, likely.

"What would I be looking for?" I ask, careful not to make it sound like I'm agreeing with her.

"That's nothing you need to concern yourself with. Just make me the photocopies. And don't let him trick you into thinking there's only one set of books. There's not, and you need to get access to it all. If you don't, well, you can wave your payday bye-bye. I will however," she adds with a roll of her eyes, "pay you a pittance slightly above Upstream's hourly rate, regardless of whether you prove yourself useful or not."

I bristle at her words, wanting to fight back and argue, but she has me right where she wants me, though not just for the reasons she expects.

The money, the freedom that would afford me? No one could rationally turn that down.

But Dimitri? I've never been able to say no to him.

"Wonderful," Rebecca smiles fondly at me, handing me a stack of documents. "I just need you to sign these, and we'll be all done."

CHAPTER 2

It's been two years, but when I see him he still manages to make me feel like a girl again.

I called, asked him meet to meet me for coffee. I figured it was the easiest way to start to get to know him again, but honestly, the thought of going through his books as a spy for Rebecca still makes me feel queasy.

Sure, I want the money.

But looking at him as he sits in the back table, staring out at the streets, I want him more.

It's not good. This mass of butterflies in my stomach, tormenting me, acting like it's totally cool for me to feel like this for him.

Well, it's not.

I try to steel myself again, but in the meantime, my eyes roam over him. He's filled out a lot in the past two years, and bulked up. Even beneath his shirt I can see the outline of his pecs, his arms huge and undoubtedly covered in a myriad of tattoos.

His hair is shorter than I remember, brushed back away from his face and revealing his strong jawline, just the hint of stubble noticeable from across the room.

I order my drink at the counter and wonder what I'm going to say. I've gone over it in my head a thousand times in the week since my meeting with Rebecca, but I still haven't a clue how this should go.

It's not like I can go in, all fists and fury for him ditching me, though that's what I want to do. He was a coward for hiding from me for so long.

But I need him on my good side.

I lick my lips as the barista hands me my coffee, and I walk towards my step-brother.

My former crush.

I'm in a skirt that hugs my curves, and the nicest tank-top I have. Red lace skirts my cleavage, my back tattoo on proud display as I sidle into the seat across from him.

He smells divine.

I have to keep myself from rolling my eyes in pleasure, instead delivering him a hard stare that slowly breaks into a smile. With him, I can't help it. I've never been able to help it. No matter how pissed he makes me, I always feel soft the second I'm with him. No matter how hard the world makes me, he tears down my defenses.

"Well hey," he practically growls as he leans in towards me.

And his voice...

It does things to me. Things I'm not proud of. Things that the quirk of his mouth makes me remember that he knows all too well.

I sit back in my chair, begging myself not to flush. Not to let those butterflies get the best of me.

It's harder than I expected.

It's one thing to try to be cool with him, be professional. To push down all the rage and anger and hatred I've felt for him over the past two years, how abandoned he made me feel. That was just the first battle.

But the second I see that smirk on his lips, all I can remember is the way his mouth tasted against mine.

I bite in on my lower lip, and he has me right where he wants me.

"Well, hey yourself," I finally say back, trying to hide my blush behind my coffee.

We stare at one another, his dark brown eyes trailing over my face, scrutinizing me, and suddenly I feel so self-conscious. He's seen me so vulnerable, so exposed, and now I just want to forget it all. For two years, I've struggled to block him from my mind, and now, here he is, looking better than ever.

"You look damn fine," he says, his grin turning lascivious, and there's no use hiding my blush.

Two years, and so many tears later, and I'm still wrapped around his fucking finger. My skirt suddenly feels too tight, my tank-top too warm, and a full body flush overtakes me.

His large hand reaches beneath the table, clamping on my knee, his fingers touching along my inner thigh, and that heat only grows.

I pull away after a moment, though. I can't let myself give into this again.

I can't give in to him again.

He raises a brow at me, but his smile tells me all I need to know. I've gone from a guarantee to a challenge, and he likes it.

It makes me sick, but I can't deny the thrill it gives me.

"This isn't about that," I say, hoping I sound curt more than turned on, but I'm way closer to the latter right now.

His grin broadens and he sits back in his chair, hands folded beneath his chin like a scolded child.

"Then what's it about, little sister?"

His reminding me of our relation tears me in two and I try to hide that down along with all my other genuine emotions.

"I just... I don't like the way things ended with us."

"I did," he growls, and that heat travels my body once more.

Just the once I'd given in to him. Just that one night, before I never heard from him again.

"You could've fooled me. You never answered any of my texts."

He shrugs as if it's no big deal.

"I had a lot going on."

"Asshole," I growl before taking a sip of my coffee. Dimitri gets under my skin like no one else could ever dream of.

And he just revels in it. That's what kills me, because I'm damned if I do, damned if I don't. If I react, he gloats. If I don't? He just pushes me further and further until I hit that tipping point.

"You love it," he says, his grin almost feral. "And besides, you had your own thing. Meeting new people, making new friends..."

"Being homeless for three days?"

"Right, that too."

I stare at him, aghast at just how easily he let that go.

"You could've fucking helped," I spit out, unable to hold it back any longer.

He lived a pampered life, an easy life, all because his mom had problems with me. I don't even know what I did. Sometimes I wonder if it was just a Snow White complex where she saw too much of my mother in me, but I doubt I'd ever get an answer.

"I could have," he agrees. "But I didn't. And now

look at you. Banging, and let me guess, a bit more rebellious than you used to be."

He leans in, and I can smell the mintiness of his breath wash over me.

"Isn't that why you called? Finally decided you wanted me to stick it to you? Get back at mommy dearest?"

His hand finds my leg again and his fingers snake up along the inner seam of my thighs, and I'd have to be a saint not to feel anything. I beg my body not to give in to that sensation of pleasure, that cruel teasing to his voice, but I can't resist it totally. Despite my anger and humiliation, he knows exactly what to say to turn me to butter.

"Fuck off," I say, but my voice is breathy and light, and he doesn't stop. We're in the middle of a crowded coffee shop in the middle of the day and he's groping me under the table.

And the worst part is how much I like it.

More accurately, how much my body likes it.

"I like it when you pretend you're mad," he growls, the pads of his fingers imprinting upon the fleshy part of my thighs. "You're so fucking hot when you act like you don't want this."

And then he pulls away, and from the smug expression on his face, I know I look as disappointed as I feel.

My breath has been stolen, and my nerves are frayed.

I just want to leave. Take off and ignore every-thing Rebecca's offered.

But it's Dimitri's offer that keeps me in my seat.

"It's not going to be like that," I say, without conviction. "I just want us to have a part in each other's life."

His grin grows and I wonder how he possibly turned my words into something dirty.

"Stop it," I insist. "I just... I was hoping maybe you could hook me up with a job or something, so we have an excuse to be around each other and reconnect."

I hope that sounds natural, though his surprised expression doesn't fill me with confidence.

"A job? That's what this is about?"

He sounds disappointed, and he leans in, his eyes narrowing.

"You know if you ever really needed money, Sarah, I'd give it to you in a heartbeat. Your stupid pride always got in the way, but you don't have to work for it."

"I'm not some beggar, Dimitri," I spit back with more acid to my tone than I expect. But it's true. I'm not going to beg for handouts when I'm able and willing to work for it.

He holds his hands up defensively.

"Whoa, Sarah, I never said you were. But we're still family."

I don't know why his words bug me so much, but

they do. For two years, we weren't family. For two years we were less than strangers, and now that he's finally back in my life, he's acting like that didn't happen? As if he's always been generous and not more than a little self-involved?

He knows he's not going to win, and he simply nods his head.

"Fine, fine. So what do you do? Still taking those weird photos?"

"They're not weird, Dimitri. They're real life."

"Sure, if that's what you want to call spying on people and taking their picture."

His smile is devious, and I know just as well as he does the time he's talking about. He was in the bath house, getting changed one day, and I snuck up to my room, leaning out my window with my camera to get a better view of him. His hard, glorious body on shameless display, thinking no one was home.

That was the day things shifted between us and his teasing ramped way up. Not even a month later, and I was kicked out.

At least we never did anything I really regretted. It isn't like I lost my *virginity* to him. Hell, I haven't lost that to anyone. Not for moral reasons, just, and I know this is cheesy, I'm waiting for the right person.

"That was one time, Dimitri."

"Sure, sweetheart, I'm sure it was the only time you caught me in the buff, but it wasn't the only time you wanted to." He licks his lower lip, his eyes narrowing at me deviously. "Tell me it's not true, and I'll hire you right now."

I stare at him, incredulous, and swallow hard. If there's one thing I'm not good at, it's lying. Especially to him. He's seen me lie about so many stupid things — and caught me so easily — he knows all my tells.

"It's not true," I say, trying to sound haughty and confident, but I'm aware of the fact that I fluttered my eyelashes too long, and he looks like he's just won a massive prize.

"I knew it," he growls, but he doesn't reach for my leg. He just lets the awkward silence grow between us until I have to look away.

"Listen, I'm a bookkeeper. I don't have school for it, but I have experience, and I'm really good. Let me help you, let me get more experience so I have something impressive on my resume. You can't get anywhere without school, and I can't get a loan since your mom is so filthy rich."

"Mm, last I heard, you liked things filthy."

"Dimitri, stop," I plead. "This is serious."

He shrugs his heavy shoulders, his shirt straining against his muscles.

"Sarah, I'm not going to leave you down and out when you ask for help. The second you called, you were going to get what you wanted. I just think you want something else more than an accounting position."

My heart leaps and for a second I wonder if he knows that I'm spying on him for Rebecca, but when that hard hand reaches to my leg, his finger teasingly running down the outside of my calf, I know he's in the dark. He just thinks I want sex.

And maybe I do.

It's so hard being a young woman and still being a virgin, and with every passing year it seems more and more significant that I still have it, and more intimidating on how to lose it. I guess most figure it out in college, but there's not a lot of opportunities when I work seventy-hours a week to barely scrape by.

"We're siblings, Dimitri. Maybe not by birth, but by chance."

That doesn't stop him, not even for a moment.

"All of the best things feel wrong the first time, Sarah. I don't hold it against you for getting scared."

"I wasn't scared!" I'm lying again.

"Don't think I forgot how wet you were against my hand, Sarah. Don't you forget how sweetly you moaned as I kissed your body, and how much you were begging for it before you suddenly *remembered the time*. You were eighteen, it's not like you had a curfew. And it was summer, no school."

I blush at the reminder, the sight of him kissing between my thighs forever burned into my memory.

"Just admit that you got off and then got scared, and we have a deal."

He's so mean!

I stare at him, swallowing as I nod.

"I was scared."

He smiles.

"Then we have a deal?" I ask, my voice suddenly foreign to me, so much softer and without much else but heated desire.

"I already said you got whatever you wanted just for asking, Sarah. Hearing you say you were scared was the icing on the cake," he says as he stands up.

He walks beside me, reaching down and touching his fingers along my jaw, making me look at him once more.

"You start tomorrow. Come meet me at my office," he says as he places his business card down on the table with his other hand. "You look much more daring today than when I last saw you," he muses before finally taking off, leaving me alone with my thoughts.

CHAPTER 3

A lready my day is off to an epic start. Firstly, it's pouring. The first real rain — not just drizzle — that we've had in weeks, and the city is more humid than ever, so my blouse is already sticking to me.

Secondly, a car splashed me as I was waiting for the bus.

And now?

"*Mr. Brokov* is not to be disturbed." The brown haired woman is staring daggers at me like I just kicked her puppy rather than simply asked to see Dimitri. She apparently takes issue with me using his first name, too, what with the emphasis on his last name.

I'm mildly surprised he went back to Rebecca's maiden name, given how she still has my father's — and my — last name. Fairfax.

"Well, it's my first day," I protest, a heavy box under my arm. I don't know what I'm going to do, not really, but I wanted to come prepared. My books, and my camera, both weigh a ton, and these heels are already killing my feet. Why did I decide that I wanted to look my best?

Why did I care so much about impressing him?

Because you have to, I remind myself, but I know it's a lie. I'm past doing things just because I have to, or just because Rebecca dangles a carrot in front of my face.

This is about me and Dimitri, and about finding out why and how he left me so casually.

The rest is just... extra.

"I know," the brunette behind the reception desk says, but her tone says she doesn't care.

"Where am I to sit?"

She ignores me, and my cheeks begin to burn. My skirt is too tight, my stockings are itchy as hell, my heels are too high, my blouse is stuck to my chest, and I feel like a hot mess.

And I'm two seconds away from throwing my box at her head when Dimitri walks in the door and it's like all the breath is just stolen from my lungs.

I've never seen him look like this. It's not just business attire, oh no. It's that the suit clings to his body, accentuating his shoulders and arms, making him seem even more filled out. His tattoos hidden away, his hair brushed and styled, and his brown eyes warm as they see me.

"Sarah," he says as he walks to me, touching his hand on my lower back and sending a shiver through me. I know it's silly but that touch seems so... significant. I can't imagine him touching his other employees in such an intimate and familiar way.

"Has Joyce seen to your paperwork yet?"

I assume that he's talking about the secretary, and I shake my head no, and she shrinks behind the desk. Great, day one and I'm already making enemies, and I have no idea what I even did to her.

"Joyce, get Sarah set up in the system right away." His tone is hard and borderline threatening. "I'll show her to her desk myself," he says and doesn't spare her another glance.

The office isn't huge, but it's still a lot to take in. I guess around fifty people must work here, most in the cubicles that litter the inner office. I expect to be led to one of the empty ones I note, but he walks beyond all of those to a door that proudly proclaims: *Mr. Dimitri Brokov, C.E.O.*.

He takes me to the smaller office just off his, pushing open the door. I almost have this feeling that it used to be for his personal secretary or something, as there's a door linking my new office right to his, but he's beaming down at me like it's a secret I'm in on.

That scares me, I'm not going to lie. I suddenly feel like it's all too fast, too soon, and way too close for comfort. Especially if I really am going to back-stab him.

And why shouldn't I? He doesn't seem apologetic in the slightest at how much he hurt me. He hasn't apologized, hasn't even pretended like he's done anything wrong, and it's eating me up inside.

I feel that well of anger begin to bubble up and I have to suppress it.

"Nice view, huh?" he asks casually, and truthfully I hadn't noticed, but he's right. It's overlooking a park, and even though we're up on the fourteenth floor, I can still hear some of the birds chirping through the glass. Ever so faintly.

"Yea, it's fine," I say, and he only looks amused at how unimpressed I'm acting. He knows what type of shitty places I've been living and working in, surely, but he lets me go with it.

"I'm just on the other side of that door, Sarah. Anytime I'm not in meetings, at least. So if you ever need help..."

I'm more aware now that his hand is still on my back, and beginning to trail lower, and all that anger dissipates like smoke and is replaced with a heat of a different kind.

We're in public, in our workplace, for heaven's sake! So why does that thought arouse me rather than repulse me? Is this really the type of reputation

I want? That I'm only getting the job because of who I am to the boss?

The thought occurs to me, unwanted. *They might not even know you're siblings. Different last names, different accents...*

Another shiver travels my spine and I push into the office, plunking the heavy box down on my desk.

"Thanks, Mr. Brokov," I say, and when I turn to face him again, he has an excited and mischievous twinkle in his eyes. I don't even want to know what put it there. I smooth out the front of my blouse and look at him, trying to make my voice stop trembling, "If you could just have someone brief me on the status of your books..."

"After how Joyce treated you back there, I doubt she's going to tell you anything accurate," he grins, and it falls into place.

Did I just steal her job?

No wonder she hates me already...

"I see," I say with a frown, licking my lips thoughtfully.

He motions his head towards the computer.

"The user login information is on the notepad, and all the programs you need are installed. The hardcopies are all kept in the filing cabinet in the back corner of my office, the keys are on your desk. Only you and I have copies, so don't lose them."

He walks in, and suddenly the office feels so much smaller and more claustrophobic, his body taking up so much space. His heat sucking up all my air.

It was one thing to see him rugged and casual at coffee, but when he's dressed like this, he looks stronger. Powerful. Like he can say anything and I'd do it, and that's a scary feeling for someone trying to resist his charms — and forget what we came so close to doing.

"If you need me," he growls, his eyes burning into mine, "you know where to find me."

And then he disappears through the door leading to his office, leaving my panties soaked, and my heart absolutely stopped.

CHAPTER 4

It's only been a week. I have to keep reminding myself of that, because honestly, I'm getting nowhere. His books are clean, though I remember what Rebecca said about him having another set. It makes sense if he's doing something shady, he'll need a clean set of books for the auditors.

Though I honestly have no idea what type of business he can be in. His company seems to be doing really well, year over year growth, and no real shady stuff. His workers seem mostly content and well paid, and there's nothing that sets off any red flags.

Though I know Dimitri is smart. Much smarter than most people give him credit for.

But what angle is he working at? And what is Rebecca hoping I'll find?

I'm taken from my thoughts by the sound of clapping and cheering, and I rise from my desk, peeking out at the cubicles.

It isn't just Joyce that's unhappy with me, I've quickly found. Everyone acts like I'm invisible, and some part of me is hurt, but another hopes it's for the better. After all, I'm not going to be here long. Six months of work, and then I'm half a million richer, I get my revenge on Dimitri, and I can do whatever I want.

Unfortunately, when I see Dimitri standing on a desk, belting out a happy birthday song to one of the employees, I'm reminded what I really want. I can't help but smile, even as I disappear back into my office and shut the door.

If they don't want me to take part in their celebrations, then I have better things to do.

Like sneak into Dimitri's office and see if he has anything else hidden that I haven't yet found.

Every other time I've come in, he's either been in the office, or the door has been open. But this time I noticed he's actually shut his door, and I know he's going to be out there for a few minutes at least. He has to eat cake if he wants to be the type of boss he projects himself to be, right?

I slip into his office, the daylight illuminating his desk just off to the side. The filing cabinet I'm familiar with is in the nearest corner of the room, opposite his desk, but there's another cabinet near the door I haven't had a chance to peek into.

There's also a shelf, though I can't imagine anything interesting being on that.

I move to the cabinet, trying to open one of the drawers, only to find it locked.

I frown, though it isn't unexpected. Anything that's going to be shady is, at the very least, going to be under lock and key.

I take out my key-ring, curious, and try with each key though none slip in. Unfortunately for my big brother, though, I learned a few things when I was desperate and scrounging for food. I pull out a bobby-pin from the side of my platinum hair, my bang instantly falling into my eyes as I remove the bits of plastic on the edges.

I move the makeshift lock-pick into the keyhole and carefully begin to shift it. I haven't picked a lock in a year or more, but all it takes is nerves of steel, and when I'm alone with no one else around? Honestly, I feel invincible. Powerful.

It's always other people's presence that brings me back to reality.

Though when I tug the cabinet and find it glides easily open, I wonder why I bother putting so much faith in their opinions anyways. I smile proudly at myself, but when I see the clutter of files, my smile is stolen.

How am I going to find anything in this mess?

There are folders that are halfway open, others thrown on top of each other, and it looks like chaos. Loose paper litters everything, and I let out a sigh.

All this work picking a lock and this is what I find?

I reach in, flicking through some of the pages when I can hear a knock on my door.

"Crap," I curse, grabbing a few pieces of paper before sliding the drawer shut and going over towards the filing cabinet that contains my work. Though then there's simply silence. Nothing.

Maybe it wasn't him after all?

I start heading back to the previous cabinet when I hear a soft vibration coming from his desk. I stop, and the sound repeats, so I walk towards it. I don't know what I'm expecting to find, and it feels weird being in his personal space without him near.

It's one thing to break into his cabinet, but his desk is more personal.

Especially when I find my hand wrapping around his phone and looking at the illuminated screen.

Incoming call: Slava Romonov

I drop the phone back to the desk and fear creeps into me.

He's involved with Slava again?

My blood grows cold and I step away, all of my thoughts of espionage fading as I walk back into my office in a stupor.

What's he doing involved with him again? Especially after the hell he went through last time?

My mouth is filled with cotton as I sit at my desk. There's another four hours left of the work day, but I have no idea how I'm going to make it through.

Not now. Not knowing the information I just found.

I was just a kid when Dimitri and Slava first started hanging out, and everyone tried to protect me from it, I guess. They didn't want me to know about the trouble they were in, but I could hear Rebecca shouting in Russian all the time at Dimitri.

I didn't know what they were into, not really. I just figured they were being boys, running around and just teasing girls or something. Not until I fell asleep in the back of my dad's truck one night and woke up to them pounding a guy's face into the pavement.

I was so naive.

Knock, knock, knock.

I startle, looking up at the door as if whoever was on the other side could see my private thoughts. I clear my throat and try to regain my composure as I shove the stolen papers into my drawer.

"Come in," I say clearly, and then there's Dimitri, his huge frame filling the doorway as he holds out a piece of vanilla cake with extra icing smeared on the side.

The dichotomy of Dimitri.

Getting calls from a thug like Slava.

Bringing me cake, just as I like it.

I wish I had more self-control than to smile at him so excitedly.

"Dimitri, you shouldn't have."

"I shouldn't have had to. Where were you? You should've come and celebrated Carl's birthday with us. I saw you there, watching me perform," he says, his brows raising and his grin growing. "You should've stuck around."

"They don't care for me," I say, trying to be nonchalant.

"Don't be silly," he says, putting the plate on my desk as he smiles down upon me. Reaching out, he touches his fingers to my forehead, pushing some of my messy, platinum waves away from my face, tucking it behind my ear. "You lose your bobby-pin?" he asks, and I'm suddenly defensive.

He can't know.

"I didn't feel like wearing one today," I say, and he simply nods his head, but I can see there's suspicion lurking beneath his brown eyes. Or maybe that's just my imagination running away with itself.

"Well, you should come out with us for drinks tonight. We're just going to kick back, and it'll be a chance for you to get to really know everyone," he says, and I am so damned tempted I could lose my mind.

But I know better than to be in the dark with him, watching as he drinks.

"I'm not twenty one yet," I remind him, and he grins.

"I know that, Sarah. But I also know a place where that doesn't matter."

I roll my eyes at him, but it's only to hide my temptation.

"I know what types of places you like to hang out in, Dimitri, and I'm not interested."

"Ah, but you don't know the types of places I like to take my employees after a long week of work, and I bet yours was a long one. Familiarizing yourself with all my accounts," he says, and his hand is still touching my hair, caressing it in a way that's so inappropriate for work.

But I'm just staring at him in shock, not knowing what to make of any of it. Of his touch, of his cruel abandonment, of his relationship with Slava...

I swallow, and my throat still feels dry and constricted, but I shake my head no.

"Another time, maybe," I say, and his hand withdraws, and all I want to do is feel those rough fingertips touching me again. It's so wrong, I can't believe it. Especially knowing what types of things he's involved in again.

"Well, if you change your mind, you have my cell," he says, and for a moment I stiffen.

His eyes narrow as he backs away, and I know I'm going to have to be a lot more cautious around him. He's known me for so long that he can tell all the littlest things about my behavior and what they likely mean.

That's the big problem with trying to spy on someone who knows me so well.

"Yea," I say, and he heads back into his office, but not without first hesitating and sending me a curious look that I don't quite know what to make of.

CHAPTER 5

*D*imitri has been acting strange for the last two weeks. Not just to me, either. Every day he comes into the office, shuts his door, and barely comes out. Even going so far as to lock the door that connects our offices a few times, leaving me unable to get the files I need to update my digital copies.

Luckily for me, the day goes quickly. Even without the whole spying aspect of the job, I'm kept plenty busy, and each day brings with it its own set of problems and concerns.

I've been so absorbed in that, and Dimitri has been so weird, that I haven't even had a chance to look at the files I stole.

But it's Friday afternoon at four thirty, and everyone is taking off a little early, so I think it's the perfect time to pull them out.

I stretch out, clearing my desk before going to my doors, locking them both. The last thing I need is someone to stumble in when I'm doing this. I then return to my desk cabinet, pulling them out. I hadn't had a chance to even see what they contain, but now I know they're graphs, of our revenue and expenses.

At a quick glance, it all looks right, balancing out at the end, and I sigh. I just broke into my stepbrother's office and stole some out of date income reports that look like they were probably headed to the shredder.

Confidential is stamped in the bottom corner, and I sigh. So much for finding anything interesting.

I push it aside and I'm just about to stand up and toss them when I look a bit closer at the date in the upper corner.

July? These are from my first week working here, and they're not the same numbers I got. I know because I always have a thing for patterns in numbers, and these aren't the same. I sit back down, scanning over the graph again, my eyebrows furrowing curiously.

Does this mean that Rebecca's right? Is Dimitri really stealing money from his own company?

From her?

It doesn't make sense.

I look at what other months are there, and find one from February. Turning to my monitor, I call up the budget for that month, and once more they don't reconcile.

It might not mean anything, I chide myself. *You're just looking for proof so that you can get your payout. This is likely just an old estimate.*

But it's stamped **Final Copy** and I can't ignore my gut instinct that there's something going on here. Especially with Dimitri being back in the company of Slava. That brute is bad news, and he's dangerous as hell.

But if he is running a money laundering scheme, who is he doing it for? And why?

Oh Dimitri, what the hell have you gotten yourself into?

CHAPTER 6

I can't ask Joyce about what I found. That woman has had it out for me since day one. I didn't realize at the time that I'd stolen her job out from under her, but ever since, she's been cold and almost cruel. Nothing that I can really report on, just things like jamming the copier before I go to use it and making me sort it out, or going to lunch and not inviting me.

Little, passive aggressive things. Plus, it's not like I haven't noticed that no one will barely look at me when she's around. I can only imagine the things she's saying about me behind my back.

But it's not my business, and I'm only supposed to be here for a short time, until I figure this Dimitri thing out. Then she can have her job back.

If there's still a job for her afterwards. It occurs to me that if she's been in on this scheme, that she could go to jail as well. Though the idea of Rebecca calling in the cops on Dimitri seems unbelievable. Truthfully, though, I never would've believed that she'd hire someone to look in on his finances either.

I pace the length of my office, back and forth. It's after eight now, but I haven't had it in me to leave. I still feel like I'm missing something. Something big.

Everyone has gone home hours ago, and the silence of the building is driving me crazy. My doors are both still shut and locked, and I'm not sure if I feel trapped or safe.

I go to Dimitri's door, touching against it gently, not sure if I want to go further. To find the things my stepbrother has been trying to hide from me behind his charming smile and crude suggestions. He promised me he was going to get out of this life, get away from the thrill of danger.

A pit forms in my stomach.

If Rebecca's right, this is way worse than him stealing money from her. Does she even know?

I don't know why I chose to sleep in the truck that night. The mansion just felt too oppressive after losing my father, and I needed to get out. It was my dad's pet project, an old truck he was in the process of restoring when he died.

I didn't realize the truck was moving, not until we

were already miles from home. It was like a dream, and through the open window, I could hear Dimitri's voice.

"Anton's fucked up for the last time." Dimitri's three years older than me, and his words send a chill through my spine. I've never heard him so angry.

"He'll be at the warehouse, dropped there by Viktor." Slava's rich, Russian accent is harder to understand, but I recognize it well. He's a bit older than Dimitri, and a lot colder. Whenever he's nearby, I feel a little ill.

"That shestyorka?" Dimitri's voice comes back, a strange, Russian word I've never heard rolling off his tongue.

"Da," Slava responds in the affirmative. "The Avtori-tyet is hoping he'll be promoted soon."

Promoted from what? To what? It's not making any sense. The wind rushes past my head, and I stay low. I don't know why I'm so scared. It's only Dimitri. He'd never hurt me.

But my gut tells me that I can't be caught. That whatever's happening tonight is something I don't want to see.

We pull up into a warehouse. It's so dark, but the shaky streetlights spill enough of its dim light along the abandoned parking lot. Concrete is half torn up, like construction had started and then got abandoned halfway through. I don't know where we are, not really, and a cold breeze nips at my skin.

Dimitri and Slava leave the truck with me still in the back and my instinct tells me they have no idea I'm here. I can't see them as they walk out of my view, but I can still hear as their steel-toed boots impact on the gravel. Their steps are slow and measured, not so much cautious as simply biding their time.

"Where'd Viktor put him?" Dimitri asks, a few feet away.

"Tied to a pole," Slava replies, and there's a pause. "There."

I want to go home. I'm scared. It's a nightmare, I know it, and I'm trying my best not to scream. I pinch my naked arm, but I don't jolt awake in my warm, comfortable bed. I'm still on the hard, ribbed flatbed of the truck, listening as Slava and Dimitri's footsteps draw further away.

What will happen if they catch me?

Dimitri would never hurt me, I promise myself, but the words are falling a bit flat, even in my mind. I never would've thought that Dimitri would be out in the middle of the night, doing who-knows-what.

"You fucking donoschik," comes Slava's growling voice, his words a mix of English and Russian. He's probably thirty feet away, but I can still hear the crack of fist impacting on a body. There's a grunt of pain, and I put my hands over my mouth to suppress a scream.

What is Dimitri doing out here? Why are they beating that man up?

Despite having lived with Dimitri and Rebecca for over three years, my Russian is still lacking at best. They rarely speak it in front of me, and when they do, their words are so foreign I can never even get enough to make sense of it.

There's another sound, fist meeting somewhere fleshier, and I curl my legs into myself. I have no idea how long we're there, losing myself in the sounds of grunts and punches, kicking and screaming.

And then the voice that I don't recognize — Anton — starts to wail in another language altogether. It's softer than Russian, more lyrical.

"Pieta!" he screams, and I wonder if it's French or maybe Italian. "Mercy! Mercy!"

The kicking stops, and Dimitri's voice is a growl, "You were supposed to bring us information on your boss, not the other way around!"

There's more kicking, and I wonder for a moment if anyone can hear us. If anyone will come to save this man from his misery. I can picture him, black and blue, bruised and hurt, and still he can only blubber half-apologies.

"They were going to kill my wife!"

"I'm going to do worse than that," swears Slava, and I can tell he means it.

What's happening? Dimitri and I live in a huge house, we have everything we could ever want. My dad had more money than he knew what to do with, and the second Rebecca came into his life, that's all she saw him for. But Dimitri and I never want for anything.

So why is he in a parking lot with a man swearing to do worse than murder *this guy's wife?*

* * *

I WAKE up in a cold sweat, staring at the ceiling. I haven't had that nightmare in years, but with all I've been seeing and hearing, it makes sense that it'd be at the forefront of my mind.

Especially after I looked up Slava and found that he'd done time after being a *Kryshas* — an enforcer — for the Russian Mob.

My stomach roils and I'm not sure what to do. I can't trust Rebecca, and I know it. I have no idea how much of this she knew, but she's never cared about me. She only kept me until I was eighteen so that she could feel the martyr after my dad died.

But if there's one person I know I can get through to, it's Dimitri. It just means I have to suck up my pride and try to get him to open up with me. No more games, no more beating around the bush.

He has to tell me what he's into, or I'll threaten to...

To what, Sarah? Go to the cops? Put him in jail? I shake my head. I know I can't do that, especially if Dimitri's working with the Mob.

Maybe it's not what it seems, I try to convince myself, but it's in vain and I know it. If he's into it with Slava and there's money missing in his company, there's no way the two aren't related. I just can't piece together how.

I slip on some jeans and a clean t-shirt. It's two in the morning, but I don't care. This can't wait anymore. It's driving me crazy, and if I can't figure it out, then Dimitri's going to help me figure it out. I just have to make him do it without exposing the fact that Rebecca hired me.

But it's not strange that a new bookkeeper noticed some irregularities and came to her boss with it, is it?

I don't have time to decide, because I'm already on the move. My roommate is already asleep, and I walk quickly to the subway, the night wrapping around me like a blanket. I love the night. I don't know what it is, and I know I should be more frightened walking alone at two in the morning, but it feels peaceful.

Serene.

I make my way to the heat of the subway tunnel and wait for the next train. I found out where Dimitri's new condo is, not far from the office, off a piece of mail he'd left on his desk. I sink into the plastic seats, and I wonder how pissed he'll be for me waking him up.

If he's even home.

Damnit, it's two in the morning on a Saturday, after all. What if he's out?

What if he's with someone? The thought makes my blood boil and I can't help but feel a little righteous interrupting him if he is with someone. A rush of possessiveness runs through me without my permission.

He's your stepbrother, Sarah. You're not supposed to

feel jealous if he finds someone. Rationally I know it's right, but it doesn't do anything for my worries, and the trip suddenly seems so long in comparison.

Just worry about what he's into, I try to remind myself, but now that the thought of him being with another woman is on my mind, it's like everything else has just stopped mattering, and all that's left is the paranoia that he really doesn't care about me.

It's not a long walk from the subway to his condo, though every step just reinforces my own anxiety. I should just turn around. Just forget this crazy endeavor. I was shaken up by my dream, by the memory of what Dimitri and Slava did to that man, but it's no reason to wake him up in the middle of the night.

But I know it's all bullshit. I'm being a coward. I want an excuse to turn around so that I can pretend none of this has happened.

I walk into the large lobby of his condo building and startle a little at the presence of a guard.

Oh no. I inwardly wince.

I had pictured marching up to his door, barging in unannounced and throwing him off guard. Somehow I'd forgotten that Rebecca may have kicked me out on my ass and taken all of my father's money, but Dimitri is a C.E.O. and still rich as sin.

Especially if he's into what I think he is.

I walk up to the security guard with his stern,

blockish face and try to give him my most charming of smiles.

"Hi, I need to be let up to room 1510."

He stares at me, not as groggy as I assumed he'd be for the late hour, and he crosses his arms expectantly.

"To see Mr. Brokov?" I add, my voice jittery, but he reaches for a phone.

I have a bad feeling about this. I should have just gone home, taken the money I made from Rebecca and just... got out of this. Got away from him.

And here I am, going to his condo at two thirty in the morning.

What do you think will happen? I chide myself, but my belly flutters with hidden excitement. Regardless of what he's into, I can't deny how he makes me feel, at least to myself. But I'll deny it to the end of the world to him.

After last time when he just ditched me like old meat? I promised myself I'd never go through that again.

So why am I filled with that weird, dark excitement? Why is my body more convinced that this is something exciting rather than terrifying?

"What's your name?" the security guard asks, breaking me from my stupor.

"Sarah," I say softly. "Sarah Fairfax."

He repeats it before hanging up the phone, motioning for me to follow him to the elevator. We walk in silence as he puts the key into the lock, hitting the 15th floor and escorting me up. The elevator ride seems so long and so short all at once, my heart pumping hard against my ribs.

I should be at home, sleeping. I should have just tried to sleep after waking up from my nightmare, not trying to convince Dimitri to come clean.

The chrome elevator doors open and unveils a ritzy hallway, filled with colorful art and muted decorations. The security guard waits for me to leave before descending back to his post.

My legs are leaden as I make my way to his condo. What am I going to say? *'Hi, Dimitri, are you involved with the Russian Mafia?'*

I shake my head.

I have to be coy.

His door is ajar when I finally get to it, but I'm afraid to push in. Once I do, there's no going back.

How strong do you think you are? I ask myself, but I sneer at the implication. I'm not a coward. I'm not going to run from this.

I push inwards and see Dimitri just at the edge of my vision, in the kitchen, and I can hear ice clinking into a glass.

I shut and lock the door behind me and he hands me a drink.

"I know you can't drink in a club, but I figure if you're waking me up at this hour, you likely need one of these." His grin is devilish, but it's not his words — nor his smirk — that steal my thoughts away.

It's the fact that he's standing before me in nothing but some loose fitted, cotton pants, and that's all. His gorgeous chest and arms are completely bared but for the litany of tattoos that mark his skin. Roses and skulls, stars and crosses, all knit together. Separate and yet part of a whole design. It's so many more than when he was younger and I'd last saw him shirtless.

I must've been staring longer than I expected, because his finger went to my chin and he guided my gaze up.

"So you've finally decided to give in?" he growls before taking all of his vodka in a single gulp, putting the empty glass on the side table. He has me practically cornered against the locked door, and I can sense his masculine heat radiating off of him.

I must've woken him because his words have a certain edge, a grittiness that I can barely resist, but I pull back.

"Dimitri," I groan, taking my own vodka into my mouth, but unlike him, I make a face as it burns down my throat.

When I open my eyes, he's still looming over me, his lips parted into a feral grin. I don't understand how he does it. During the day he looks professional, clean cut and put together.

But here in the privacy of his home, shirtless and

eyes lit with hunger, it's another side of him alto-gether. One that drives me wild.

He's dangerous, Sarah, I plead with myself to remember, but my thoughts are muddied by his presence, and already my resolve is wavering, so the only thing I can do is call back on that anger that I've had within me for over two years.

I push past him and finish my drink, leaving my emptied glass on the table. The alcohol makes my tongue a little looser, and I spin to look at him.

"You can't treat me like this," I say, my voice taking on a venomous tone I'm not used to, but he just looks amused.

I hate it. He should be feeling bad, feeling upset at himself, at me, at whatever.

So why does he look so damned amused?

"Treat you like this? You mean, allow you to barge into my home, unannounced, at two in the morning?"

Well, when he says it like that...

I have so much anger in me busting to get loose, though, and logic can't possibly fight that.

"Ever since I started working for you, you've barely even seen me except to torment me," I say, and there's hurt creeping into my voice. And I know it's not even all true. He's seen me plenty. But it's not enough. It's not what I hoped for when I let him back into my life.

I don't know what I wanted, but it wasn't this.

"Ahh," he says, padding towards me in his bare feet. "So my little sister is feeling neglected when she's just another employee?" he says, more than asks, and suddenly my back is up against the bar, staring up at him.

How does he keep cornering me?

"I don't want to be treated any different," I protest, but I know it's a lie, and from the way his grin is growing, so does he.

His hand goes to my throat, his thumb pressing against the hollow as his brown eyes bore into mine.

"That sounds like you want to be treated different," he coos, and my nipples stiffen. I wish I'd worn a bra, but I had been in such a rush, and now the faint outline of my arousal was embarrassingly visible.

I can't think with his rough hand pressing into me, but his presence is suffocating and I can't get away.

"I don't," I feebly protest, but my heart is racing so fast I can barely make sense of my thoughts. I never should have come here. I should've stayed curled up in bed.

His other hand reaches out, touching along my hip, creeping up under my t-shirt.

"So why are you here, Sarah, begging for me to stop tormenting you?" His eyes are lit with lust, and he moves in towards me so that his body is nearly touching mine. I can remember so vividly the last time he had me in a position like this, and the things he did to make my body sing.

But I swore to myself I'd never let that happen again after he left me broken hearted the morning after.

I slap his hands away and stalk to his living room, spinning about to glare at him.

"I'm not some disposable toy you can play with and forget about, Dimitri, despite what you may think!"

He laughs as he pursues me, like an animal playing with his prey.

"That's not what happened last time," he says, and he keeps walking towards me as I keep backing up. My ass presses against the couch's armrest, and I'm forced to stop as he moves even closer. "And you can't tell me you didn't enjoy it."

A flush goes across my cheeks, and I know he's right. I did enjoy it until the next morning, and then everything was a mess. The memory brings a heat to my body that isn't welcome, though. I'm trying to remain strong, to confront him about... what?

About the money, I remind myself, but I know that isn't what this is about. The money could've waited until Monday.

The truth of the matter is the memory of him and Slava beating up that guy made my body wet. It filled me with anger and arousal that I haven't felt in years, and I needed to see him before logic could kick in.

"I didn't," I lie to him, and he grabs a fist full of the front of my t-shirt, tugging me near him as he glares down at me.

"Then why'd your lip twitch?" he asks and I regret lying to him. He knows how I look when I lie. The little, hidden tells that no one else knows to look for, but he does.

"Nothing," I murmur, but I'm losing. I know I'm losing.

I want to lose.

Maybe that's what this is all about. Losing. Giving into passion. Letting myself feel something so intensely once more.

He steps closer, and my torso bends back over the couch, held there so precariously as his legs press between mine.

"Why'd you really come here, Sarah?" he growls, and the words remind me of just how wrong this is. For years we lived under the same roof, growing up together.

Why does he make my blood run so hot, then? Why can't I deny how badly I want him? Why didn't I ever find another man I was interested in?

His free hand snakes up my side once more.

"If you want me to stop, just say the word," he grins, and I know the word he's referring to instantly. It was a silly thing we came up with when we would wrestle as kids. A childish safeword. *Uncle.* That's all I have to say to admit defeat and get him to back off.

So why doesn't the word come to my mouth immediately as his rough hand starts teasing up over my delicate ribs, playing them like an instrument? My eyes flutter shut and I try to back up, but there's nowhere to go.

"Stop," I murmur, the sound so lusty.

His lips go to my ear, warm breath washing over it, "That's not the word."

My fingers dig into the leather upholstery of the sofa and I tip backwards, but he catches me, his hand going to my thigh and holding me there as he shifts in and I feel that throbbing heat against me. Separated by cotton and denim, but nonetheless, it's there, and it's burning for me.

We never went all the way, and I swore to myself I'd never be in a situation like that with him again, but I'm helpless to stop.

He might be in the mob, I beg myself to remember. *Beating people up is just the beginning. He's a* monster *Sarah.*

But my body doesn't seem to care. I need him. Just one night, just to get him out of my brain. To forget all of those what-could-have-beens from circling in my mind for the next two years. Even if he broke my heart, he's still claimed it, and this is the only way to reclaim it, I feebly argue with myself.

He grinds against me, and I know he thinks he's winning.

He knows he's winning.

My protests are getting so weak and pathetic, but when his mouth crashes against mine, and I can taste the vodka on him, my world suddenly feels peaceful. Like the eye of the storm. Knowing it still swirls around me, and yet I have a moment of bliss in the middle of torment.

My tongue presses against his, eager to taste him, to feel his lips and tongue tango with mine.

"You know I like it when you pretend you don't want this," he growls and I'm losing myself to him, and fast. I've no thoughts left but for that throbbing member pinned between us, the way my legs are spreading around him.

I swallow, and his mouth is on mine once again, and suddenly the tempest within rages. There's no holding it back anymore, no hiding just how turned on I am.

He lets go of my thigh and his hand travels beneath my shirt, finding my bare breasts beneath. He lets out a moan that reverberates through me, and I can't help the fact that my nipples stiffen, prodding his hard digits.

"You should've given in earlier," he says, tugging on my nipple in a teasing, playful manner that belies his hard muscles and deadly gaze.

I'm scared. I'm scared of him, of what he's into. There's no denying that.

But even more frightening is how those fears ignite my passions rather than extinguishing them.

I moan and there's nothing that I can do to hide it as I wrap my legs around his waist, feeling him begin to gently grind against me. I've seen him nude before, spied on him as he changed, grazed my fingers against it the last time I saw him, but this is something new altogether.

The fire between us hasn't dimmed at all, and instead, is burning hotter than ever.

He bites my lip, tugging on it, and that little spark of pain leaves me shivering.

"Tell me you want it, Sarah," he growls, and punctuates his words with an extra little grind.

My mind is a haze, filled with lust and arousal. He's my step-brother, my boss, and I know this is all so fucking wrong. I should run away from him, from his mother, from all this shit that's come into my life because of them.

But instead, I'm moaning out the words, "I want you," and sounding like a craven beast.

I have to stop this. I have to stop before this goes too far, before I go too far. I'm losing my mind, and he's the culprit, but he's making me burn like wildfire and when he pushes me back onto the couch, I feel so small. So delicate in his brutish grasp.

His weight presses down on me, and he's solid

muscle against me, pinning me into the soft, leather couch.

His mouth trails down my throat, peppering kisses there, and I'm breathing hard, struggling not to get wrapped up in how his kisses send sparks from my stomach, down to my clit.

"Stop," I gasp again, his stubble running down between my clavicles, his fingers pulling down my shirt as his mouth heads towards my swollen, pink nipple. I'm so turned on, it's ridiculous. It feels like my panties have melted off, and I arch my back as he refuses to listen to me.

Because you didn't use the word, I chide myself, but even knowing that, I'm reluctant to say it.

I don't want him to stop.

His fingers work the button on my jeans, and I'm so close to that edge of no return. I can just do it. See what I missed out on two years ago, feel him take my virginity from me.

Heat builds in my stomach with such intensity as I think about what his hands and body would feel like, claiming me for his own.

Does he even want that? You're just a conquest. Forbidden fruit that means less than nothing to him.

That thought is the one that brings that terrible word to my lips.

"Uncle," I gasp out, just as I feel his fingers brush against the top of my panties, and then it all stops. He pulls away from me, standing and staring down at me with quickened breath and a desperate throbbing beneath his thin, cotton pants.

His eyes are stormy and dangerous, and even though he's stopped, it looks like he's barely restraining himself. Like he's just going to throw himself on top of me and take me anyways.

But then he turns back to the bar, pouring himself up a vodka. The hard lines of his muscles are more prominent, the tattoos along his back stretched taut with his tension.

"Here's a hint, Sarah. You show up at two in the morning for a booty call and then withhold the booty, bad things happen. You're just lucky—"

"Lucky *what*?" I hiss at him as I leap from the couch, fixing my jeans buttons and shirt as I glare at him. All my lust and desire still runs molten through my veins, but now it's turned to rage. "Lucky you don't force yourself on me?"

He spins, his hand grasping my shoulder as he glowers down at me, pointing at me with the glass still in his hands.

"I would *never* hurt you, Sarah," he swears with so much conviction I'd believe him — that is, if he didn't leave me broken hearted before.

"Hah!" I laugh, not buying his delusions. Not this time. "Like you didn't hurt me last time?"

"If you remember, I was the one that left unfulfilled last time," he says, his grasp not lightening on my shoulder.

"I was *scared*, Dimitri! We're not supposed to happen. That was never supposed to happen."

"What, it's okay for you to spy on me, take pictures of me naked, but the second I show interest in you, it's suddenly wrong?"

My skin grows hotter, and I know my face must be a bright red. Anger and embarrassment battle for dominance.

"I was wrong to take pictures of you," I say through gritted teeth.

"Damn fucking right you were."

"You were wrong not to call me after... after we hooked up."

"I told you," he says with narrowed eyes. "Things got busy."

"What the fuck could possibly make you forget I exist for two years?" I yell, tears threatening to spill. I blink faster, begging myself not to lose my cool, but it's a battle that I can't win.

He softens a little, that tough guy act melting back into the side of Dimitri I used to know so well. That gentleness, the desire to protect me. I knew — before I was kicked out — that he'd have done anything to protect me. But he proved me wrong.

"If I could have done anything not to cut you out of my life, I would have," he swears, and his conviction...

I believe him.

Don't be stupid, Sarah, I plead with myself, but I

want so badly for him not to have hurt me as bad as he did.

"You broke my fucking heart," I sob, and I can see him cringe. He doesn't brush it off this time, doesn't act like those words don't cut through him, and his hands loosen on my shoulder.

"I shouldn't have let you get wrapped back up in me," he says, and the words make me bristle. As if he knew this is how it would all play out, that I'd find myself lusting for him once more. "I never should've hired you on. Just let you go do your thing, live your life."

The dam has broken and tears stream down my cheeks.

"Are you firing me?"

He sighs, leaning against the bar, his back facing me. "I should."

A sob makes me hiccough, and there's a burning sensation in my lungs. I can't catch my breath, so many emotions spinning through me that I can barely feel one before it's replaced with another.

"Don't," I whimper, reaching out and touching his wrist. What am I doing? I should just let him do it. Rebecca will be pissed at me for not going through with it, but there's nothing I can do if Dimitri decides to fire me.

"I can't," he says, and he sounds so defeated and exhausted. Maybe not seeing my face makes it easier to talk honestly, without all of his cruel teases and smart-ass jabs. "When I saw you in the coffee shop, you looked unreal. Like out of a dream," he sighs.

I stand behind him silently, withdrawing my hand, but he captures it in his and he tugs me in against him, forcing my hand to his chest as he turns back around.

He guides my fingers, and I find a pucker in his skin, a strange scar I hadn't noticed in the dim light. "Do you know what this is?"

"No," I whisper.

"It's a bullet wound," he says, releasing my hand. "There's another on my back." I step back and, true to his words, there's another scar. So small, yet it leaves me with such a feeling of dread.

What's he gotten himself into?

He turns and looks down at me, his gaze a stormy sea.

"I'm going to fuck your life up if you let me," he swears, and those words send a jolt of excitement and fear through me. "I'm not going to lie. I want you. Need you. But I can't have you, not without repercussions."

"We knew that already," I say, trying to hold in my emotions. "We knew we could never be a thing. Rebecca... she'd flip. And... it's wrong," I manage, and he reaches out, his fingers coiling through my hair.

"It's more than that," he says with a scowl, but he's looking at my lips, as if he can't tear his eyes away. "It's dangerous."

"Let me help," I say softly, but he shakes his head, and I know this is one point not worth arguing.

I step backwards, away from his touch, away from the temptations he's risen within me.

"I gotta go," I mutter, grabbing my purse, and he doesn't fight.

The door slamming behind me reverberates through the hall, and I stand on the other side of the door.

What just happened?

CHAPTER 7

I haven't been able to get the taste of his lips off mine. I know it's all in my head, that his taste couldn't have permeated my body so easily, but I swear, I lick my mouth and all I can think of is his.

I don't know what I regret more — going over there in the first place, or leaving. I can't get him out of my head, the dark warnings, and burning passion between us. Maybe it's all in my mind. Maybe to him I really am just off limits and so he wants to have me. He has everything else, after all. The nice house, the good job.

The criminal enterprise.

The thought is like a dagger to my heart. Why did this have to get so complicated? I was prepared for him stealing from his mother. I might have even liked that.

But this is something so much deeper.

I still haven't told Rebecca about what I've found, because what if it's nothing? I've seen her temper flare, and I know better than to come to her with bad information.

"Earth to Sarah." Joanna snaps her fingers in front of my face and my eyes slowly refocus on my roommate. We're sitting across from one another, and we're supposed to be catching up. Our silly, weekly ritual. Both of us tend to get stuck in our own heads — and rooms — more than is healthy, so our compromise was Saturday dinners together.

"Sorry," I mutter, rubbing my head and forcing a smile at her. "You're setting up a new data center?"

"Yup," she says proudly, putting aside her own confusion at my behavior for the time being. "It's a pretty big deal, a big promotion. I mean, it's not like it's really that much fun, but it's better than most things they have me do in IT."

"That's great," I say with manufactured enthusiasm. Joanna's been a great roomie, but I know her passion is definitely not in the infrastructure side of IT. She prefers the more hands-on aspects, and I know she was gunning for a background check job in HR but was turned down. Not enough experience, they said.

"Yea. I mean, this might be a real shot at doing something and climbing the corporate ladder," she says, spearing a piece of broccoli and chewing it thoughtfully. "Plus, if I can set it all up, then I'll know all the back end stuff," she grins mischievously and I can't help but laugh.

"So what's been going on in that blonde little head of yours, Sarah? Did I actually hear you stumble in at five in the morning today?"

She heard that? Oops.

"Uh, yea. It wasn't... It was nothing." I can't fight the flush traveling up my cheeks. It so wasn't nothing. I wish I didn't blush so easily when I'm caught in a lie.

"Uh-huh. You got a boy, finally? I've been telling you — for how long? — you need to get out and date. So why are you all gun-shy about it? I think it's fabulous," she says, twirling her fork in the air.

Joanna's hair is pulled back in a ponytail, her dark-rimmed glasses falling down on her nose a little and I can't help but laugh despite all the craziness.

"He's not a boy," I say defensively, and that just makes her smile broaden.

"Ohh, a man, then?"

"He's nothing. It's nothing. Just my boss, he needed something."

Her brow raises and I wonder if I said too much.

"At ass-o'clock on the morning?"

"It was important."

"On a Saturday morning?"

"Really important?"

She rolls her eyes, "Girl, I know a booty-call when I hear it, and if he's calling you up on a Saturday night, then the help he needs isn't going to be *that* type of important. You got a thing for him or something?"

I'm suddenly grateful that I didn't tell her that he's my stepbrother, because it gives me a chance to gush a little.

"Yea, I guess. It wouldn't work, though."

"Well, yea, that's kind of sexual harassment."

"It's not like that. I mean..."

She stares at me, waiting.

"He didn't... really call. I just went over."

I swear, it looks like she's going into shock, and I can't help but feel a little proud. I doubt I've ever told her anything that has truly shocked her, even when I told her about spying on that guy down the street and turning him into the cops for abusing his little boy. Had the pictures to prove it.

"Wow," she utters, and my pride swells. "I didn't know you had it in you. So what'd you do?"

"Nothing. Not... not really. He offered me a drink, and then... he kissed me."

"He kissed you?" She's leaning in, her food forgotten as she stares at me intently.

I nod, and remember his lips crushed against mine, the weight of his body over me. I wanted nothing more than to forget about the world and our obligations and worries, to lose myself in a night of passion with him, but maybe the chasm is too wide. Maybe he hurt me too bad, and he's in too deep.

If anything can turn me from him, the thought that he might be involved with the Russian Mafia should have me running, right?

"But I left before anything more could happen," I add on and she looks disappointed.

"Oh."

"It's not right, is it? He's my boss. And, oh God, I have to go see him again Monday."

"Yea, that's going to be weird. Do you think it'll happen again?"

And I honestly don't know how to answer her.

CHAPTER 8

This is quite possibly the stupidest thing I've ever done in my life. I mean, it's definitely top three, at the very least.

I'm sitting in an abandoned building, surrounded by peeling paint and rusted beer cans, the stink of vomit thick in the air. I'm afraid to even touch anything, both of my hands wrapped around the lens of my camera.

It's an overcast day, fortunately, since that way the light won't reflect off my camera lens as easily, but it's locking in all the humidity, and I can feel the rain threatening to fall.

The window I'm staring out of is broken, but it gives me a perfect view of my target. A little cafe across the street that I thought was abandoned until I watched Dimitri knock and go inside. I scrambled up into my vantage point once I knew that's where he was going, but I can't make sense of it.

I don't even know what it was that made me want to tail him today. Something about the way he's been acting, about the way he looked. I figured immediately it had something to do with Slava, but I don't know what or how.

You're grasping at straws, I tell myself, and somewhere I feel that's true, but my gut instinct says I'm onto something, and I have to see it through. It's better to look and find out that I'm wrong than never look at all, right?

There's no movement from inside the store, and I let out a bit of a sigh. I can't get a good look at who Dimitri's inside with, I have no idea what they're talking about. This is just a complete waste of time and I know it.

For days I've been keeping my distance from him, and he's been respecting it much to my chagrin. Maybe I want to be pushed a little. Maybe I want to just have that responsibility of choice stolen from me for a little while so that I won't have to feel guilty about my feelings for him.

I lift the camera to my eyes again, looking through the zoomed out lens to the upstairs apartments, but the curtains are all drawn. That, in and of itself, is weird. The windows are all closed but it's sweltering outside, and the curtains are still on the windows so it's not abandoned. I don't know why but curtains always seem to be the first thing that goes when a place is abandoned.

I sigh, pointing my viewfinder down to the main entrance. Still nothing.

My calves burn from staying squat like I am, but I can't move. I know the drill only too well. If I move, if I draw attention to myself, I get caught. I have to be slow and cautious, keeping my mind on the task at all time.

So that means no fantasizing about Dimitri.

Lightning cracks in the distance and I gasp, a scuttle behind me making me fall backwards onto my ass.

Real smooth, I think to myself as I push myself up from the dirty floor. I'm going to need a shower after this.

A few moments later and thunder booms.

Oh shit, I think, *I can't get stuck in a downpour.* I'm six blocks from work and I didn't bring my umbrella.

But to my disappointment, the heavens don't listen to my protests and instead open up, heavy, hard rain splattering on the pavement. It's only a second later that I see the door open.

I raise my camera back to my face, snapping as quickly as I can, hoping to get a picture of the person Dimitri was meeting with, but he stays hidden in the dark recesses of the store. Dimitri hails a cab almost instantly, and leaves me behind in the rain tortured streets.

I lean forward and let out a sigh. *Another bust.*

I don't have cash for a cab, but I have to get back soon. My lunch break is almost over.

Glancing down at the streets, looking over the people as they hurry out of the torrential downfall, I lament my luck. Splatters of rain come in through the cracked window, sprinkling my face and cheeks in its warm wetness.

I'm just about to stand up and leave, resign myself to getting soaking wet, when a man catches my eye. He looks familiar. His hat covers most of his face, his jacket pulled up over his head, but I bring my camera back up and zoom in.

My fingers go cold, my body beginning to tremble, but I still hit the shutter button on my camera a dozen times before the man enters the same building my brother just left.

Slava.

If there was any doubt in my mind before now, it's completely erased now.

CHAPTER 9

I shut the door to my office, my blouse and skirt clinging to my body from the wetness. I feel — and look — like a drowned dog, and I probably smell just as bad.

I debated even coming back. If Slava and Dimitri are visiting the same abandoned store, there's definitely something going on between them. Something big.

I just don't know what it is.

Leaning against my desk, I try to catch my breath and make sense of my jumbled thoughts, but it's useless. What can I make sense of? Once you get in with the Mafia, there's no getting out, is there? I had hoped that Dimitri's brief brush with criminality was a phase, something he would grow out of.

The scope of what he was involved in started to dawn on me, though, and all those little things he's said to me, all the things I've seen, all started to slide into place.

It's too much to deal with and I grab my camera and purse, heading for my door when the door from Dimitri's office suddenly slides open.

"Sarah, I—"

He stops talking as he looks over my soaking body, amusement sparkling in his eyes. He doesn't look any different, any more changed. Same old Dimitri, unable to take anything serious.

"Well, looks like you took a swim on your lunch break."

My heart protests, pounding against my chest.

He's your stepbrother, but he's dangerous, I tell myself, but seeing that wicked glint to his eyes, my body feels the magnetic pull to him once more.

What's wrong with me?

"Yea, I got caught in the rain," I say, my breath so high in my chest, my fingers trembling as I clutch my camera. His gaze drops to my purse, then my camera, tilting his head to the side.

"Taking pictures in the rain?" Suspicion runs in his voice and I curse myself for being so careless. I shouldn't have been taking off in the middle of the day anyways, but I just can't breathe in here. I can't make sense of it.

"Something like that," I say, shrugging my purse higher up my shoulder. "I'm not feeling well, so I was going to take off early."

"Were you?" he asks, daring me to repeat myself, and I shrink like a scolded child. He's only a bit older than me, but he seems so much larger than life.

He takes a step closer to me when I don't answer, placing a file on the corner of my desk. It's the closest he's been since that night in his apartment, and my body is craving his. My skin ignites when he brushes his fingers along my cheek, my eyes fluttering as I lean into it despite it all.

Why am I so pulled towards his darkness?

"You feel chilly," he says, suddenly seeming concerned, and he takes my camera from my hand, setting it on the desk. "Are you sure it's just the rain?"

Can he see that something's wrong? Can he read me so easily?

I shake my head, and his presence is suffocating me. I'm drowning in him, and the worst part is how little I want to fight it. When I'm away from him, I can think clearly. I know what a bad idea this all is.

But the second he returns to my side, I turn to putty.

His fingers lace into my hair, pulling back the wet strands, his eyes looking at me intently.

"You can't lie to me, Sarah. You never have. So tell me what's really wrong. Is it the thing at the condo still?"

I shake my head, feeling the little tug against my scalp.

He smiles, a moment of triumph passing over his face.

"Well, then tell me," he says, his lips lingering closer to mine. He's so much taller than I am, yet somehow he feels so near, like if I just leaned up on my toes a little, I could turn off my mind again. Lose myself in his body, if only for a second.

"I saw you," I say with a little whisper, my brows knit in the center. "I know you're into something, Dimitri. Something bad."

He raises his brows but I'm not sure I surprised him. His free hand finds my hip.

"Where did you see me, Sarah?" he asks, and his tone is darker than I've ever heard it. Gone is the teasing, the lightness. Instead, he's simply the cold devil I only ever saw that once, in the parking lot so many years ago.

"In the cafe," I murmur, and I can't look at him anymore. I don't know if it's shame or what, but I feel like I'm the one that's been disobedient.

His fingers tighten in my hair and he makes me meet his gaze. "You saw me... walk into a building?"

I nod.

"And where were you?"

"Across the street."

"And you took pictures of me in the building?"

I nod again.

He curses under his breath, and glares down at me.

"Didn't you learn what happens to you when you take pictures of me when I don't know you're there?" he says, and the edge of warning to his voice sends icy-hot chills down my spine.

He's scaring me.

He's turning me on.

I swallow, and I know I have to choose my words carefully. Though I don't know what to say, especially not something that's going to get me out of hot water with him. I bite in on my lower lip, watching as the anger boils behind his dark eyes.

"Sarah," he says through clenched teeth, and I cringe.

His hand squeezes my hips, his other moving from the nape of my neck to the hollow of my throat, his thumb pressing against it in warning, and even though I know he wouldn't kill me, I still feel a rush of fear.

"I'm sorry," I say, louder than I anticipated. "I'm worried for you."

His expression is at war, and he pulls back a half-inch.

"You should be worried for you," he says, his jaw clenched. "You don't have a clue what trouble you could've gotten into today, Sarah. No *fucking* idea. If they knew you were spying, you'd be gone in a second. Not even a chance to regret your bone-headed actions." He releases me, backing up and throwing his hands up in exasperation. "I should've known you wouldn't be able to leave well enough alone."

I take a step back, my shoulders pressed into the wall and he comes towards me again, all fire and brimstone. I cringe away, but then his lips crash against mine as if he owned them, his tongue probing my mouth. I'm in shock, and a rush of excitement goes through me. My door is unlocked, anyone could simply barge in.

So why does that make it hotter rather than scarier?

"You should've stayed away from me," he says, his eyes smoldering beneath his dark lashes as he cups my jaw. He's stolen my breath, and there's something in his expression that chills me to the bone.

I suck in air, but then I capture his mouth with mine again, and we're a tangled mess of limbs. He doesn't seem to care that I'm still soaking wet and ruining his perfect suit, especially not as he lifts my thighs, pressing my back into the wall. He has me pinned, my arms tossed around his neck, and I'm not sure if it's passion or fear that's binding us together at this point in time.

It's wrong, but it feels so right, and for once, I succumb. I let my mind simply drift, losing myself in the pleasure of his hard body tensing against mine.

"You never should've tempted me," he growls darkly. "You are sweet." He pulls back glancing at my face, "You're still pure, *da?*" he asks, and when I nod my head, he lunges for my throat, his tongue exploring the delicate bones. There's nothing in the world better than that sensation, and I have to hold in a sigh of pleasure.

"We were both safer before you came back," he says, his teeth nipping my collarbone, half possessive, half teasing. "We were better off."

"I wasn't," I protest, my fingers running into his hair, my back arching towards him, my nipples stiffened beneath my bra. "Every day I missed you."

"This is about more than you and me," he says, even as his fingers move up my thighs, digging into my ass, groping me with wild abandon in my office. "If you want this, it's all or nothing."

And I want it.

"All or nothing," I say out loud, finishing my silent thought. I grind against him, and he reaches for his belt.

"There's no going back. After this, you're mine," he says, and the word burns in my belly, my stomach suddenly filled with potent fireworks exploding in time to his heartbeat.

My lips press against his once more as I moan against him, feeling his belt slip open, the jingled sound delighting all of my senses.

In his office there's a vibration, his phone purring on his desk, but he ignores it as he hikes up my skirt.

"This what you want, Sarah?" he asks, his voice heavy with lust, taking on such a rich, enticing tone, and I nod like a schoolgirl afraid of speaking. He reaches up beneath my skirt, grabbing the edge of my panties and beginning to tug them downwards.

"Dimitri," I moan, my head tilting back, my body aching and throbbing with desire. "I've thought about this for so long."

"Since you ran from me?"

"I wish I hadn't," I admit, and my body warms with the thought of him taking me back then. Claiming me for his own years ago. How different things could have been.

His mouth sucks on my throat, and I know I'm going to have a bruise there, but it feels so damn good I don't care. I just want more. His hand tugs down my panties, unleashing my heat, and his fingers find the warm silk there and presses in.

I gasp, my eyes rolling back in my head at the unexpected pleasure. All the anxiety and fear that has welled up inside of me seems to be focused in that one bundle of nerves. He strokes it so expertly, drawing out more and more of my juices until I'm thoroughly coated and then reaches for his cock, pressing the crown against me. He teases me with that flared head, and I know it's wrong how much I want it. I know it's sinful how good he feels, but all I can manage is a moan of pure delight.

Knock-knock-knock-knock.

The sound is urgent, and for a second, I wonder if it's in my head. Only now do I realize the sound of an incessant phone ringing has been going on for some time from his office. When Dimitri drops me to the ground, though, quickly stuffing his swollen cock back in his pants and moves towards his own office, I know it's not a hallucination.

He closes the door to my office, and I can make out mumbled sounds of him talking to someone in his office.

When he returns, his face is somber, no longer holding the heat it had just a moment ago.

"Someone... Someone's killed mom."

CHAPTER 10

There's a buzzing in my ear and I can't fully make sense of the words coming out of the detective's mouth.

Dimitri is at my side, his arm draped around me, my eyes puffed up and swollen. Everything that'd happened between us in the office had been instantly forgotten in a mess of tears and frantic sobbing. Dimitri hasn't cried, though. If anything he's become harder, as if in the span of the last few hours, he's grown a decade.

"We deserve to know," he's saying, his hand clutching my arm. "We're her kids."

"It's a delicate situation. We don't have all the information yet, so we need to ask a few more questions. The better you can help us, the faster we can resolve this."

Dimitri's jaw clenches, but he nods.

"Do you know if your mother had any enemies?"

"My mother owned many companies, was on the board of two groups, and had more power than most in New York," Dimitri says with a mix of pride and agitation. "You don't get to her level without making some enemies."

"Any that could do something like this?"

Dimitri shakes his head, his lip pulled into a sneer.

"Of course not. Corporate tycoons are willing to ruin you in a dozen ways but murder isn't high on their list."

I sob, and Dimitri squeezes me tighter, leaning in and whispering in my ear, "Go into the guest room, Sarah. I can finish this up and I'll tell you anything important."

I'm too weak and exhausted to argue, and so I stand and give a teary nod to the detective before I make my way down the hall.

I shut the door behind me and go to the pristine, white bed, collapsing into it. I know Rebecca and I didn't have the best relationship, and I've thought about her being gone more than once, but never like this. My heart was breaking for Dimitri, and I hate myself for being so weak that I'm reduced to a simpering mess.

Maybe it's just the intensity of the day, of how it happened.

Of how much it reminds me of when my father was killed.

I was so young, but the pain stabs through me like it was just yesterday. The fear, the vulnerability, the pain, it all floods through me, and I'm devastated once more. I was just a girl, abandoned by the only biological family I had. Rebecca inherited all of my father's fortunes, and I was left to her mercy.

Dimitri was the only reason I was able to get through it, and now I know I have to be strong. To help him through this loss.

But when I sit up, wiping away the tears, trying to collect myself, I can't bring myself to face them. I walk to the dresser, looking into the mirror at my disheveled platinum hair, my stormy, blue eyes, and the redness beneath them. I'm so pale that my sorrow stands out like a sore thumb, and I open the drawers, looking for a spare box of tissues.

The guest room mostly contains old linens that are past their prime, though in the bottom drawer I find something that I thought had been lost. A golden locket that had belonged to my biological mother. My breath hitches as I open it up, seeing the small picture of us as a family.

I was only ten or eleven in the picture, the edges a bit worn and faded, and I look at my mother's face. She was so beautiful, so vibrant, and I have to close it once more. A couple years later and she had passed away from the cancer that ravaged her.

I close the locket with a faint click and slip it into my blouse pocket, finding the box of tissues I'd been searching for. I dab my eyes free of their tears, and take a deep breath.

"Be strong. Dimitri needs you," I tell myself in the mirror. There's still a sob trapped in my chest, but helping him is more important than getting stuck in mourning for people I lost years ago. Rebecca didn't deserve what happened to her, but it was the reminder of my own parent's death that was truly haunting me.

I plaster a fake smile on my face. I once heard that if you smile, even if you don't want to, that you'll start to feel a bit better. Unfortunately, that little upward pull on my lips did little for my mood, and even less for that pit in my stomach. I remember all too well how inconsolable I was after mom died, and that was natural.

How angry I was after dad died?

Dimitri must be feeling that ten-fold.

I'm about to push open the door to rejoin Dimitri and the detective when there's a knock on the wood.

"Sarah?" Dimitri's voice sounds harder than ever, and I open the door to look at his steely face.

"The detective's gone for now," he says, his eyes roaming over my face, and I hope I don't look as terrible as I did moments ago. His hand reaches up, touching along my jaw, and for a split second I remember what we'd done in my office just moments before we found out the horrible news and a heat floods through me.

It's not appropriate, I remind myself, referring to both the act itself and the memory coming back to me.

"Are you okay?" he asks, some of that gentleness returning to his voice, and his dark eyes meet mine.

"I was just about to ask you the same thing," I admit, my gaze dipping down. "I'm sorry for freaking out."

"Don't be sorry," he says. He moves in and I catch a whiff of his cologne in the air. "This... It's going to be a hard few days."

"When can we start making arrangements?"

"We won't be able to do the funeral until they perform..." he trails off, but I know the drill. They have to do the autopsy first, and that could delay the funeral by a few days at least.

"We'll need her will."

He nods. "Her lawyer's already been called. She'll be meeting with us later to go over mom's wishes."

"Dad's plot..." I trail off when I feel my voice breaking.

"I know. He wanted them on either side of him. His two special ladies," Dimitri replies, tucking some of my stray hair behind my ear. "You don't have to worry about this, Sarah."

"I'm not sixteen anymore," I say with a sigh, but

inside, I feel like I may as well be. I'm not prepared to deal with this, not again.

Why does everyone I love have to die so tragically? I'd gone through this all before. The detectives, the constant questions and dead ends, the uncertainty. I lost my father, and we never found his killer. And now the only family I have is Dimitri.

My eyes meet his once more. Dimitri. The man I was so close to losing my virginity to. The man that has haunted my dreams and my fantasies for years.

The one man that's supposed to be off limits to me.

He's looking at me so seriously, studying me with this strange edge to his dark gaze. I can't get a read on his emotions or how he's feeling, just this strange sense that things aren't right. His jaw is set hard, the little bit of stubble making him look a bit darker and more disheveled. He's run his fingers through his hair a few too many times and now it's sticking up in places, making him seem a little more manic.

He looms over me in the doorway, and for a long time, we don't say anything. His hard fingertips run along the shell of my ear, and it's both soothing and scary in a way. His eyes rarely move from my face, and the air grows thick between us.

"I know what you were doing for Rebecca," he says quietly, breaking the extended silence, and a chill goes up my spine. His voice is... off. Ominous and yet emotionless at the same time.

"I don't know what you're talking about," I say, but I can't meet his eyes when I lie to him, and he can see right through me.

His index finger lifts my chin upwards, and for a second I wonder if he's going to kiss me, but when I see his narrowed eyes, I know I'm not that lucky.

"Don't lie to me, Sarah. Don't ever lie to me."

I flinch. He's pissed.

"I know what you were doing for Rebecca. And you and I are going to go through this shit with the detectives, and we're going to tell them nothing about that, right?"

I nod my head, but there's a pit of dread in my stomach. Dimitri couldn't have had anything to do with this. He'd never hurt his own mother.

His own mother who was using her stepdaughter to spy on her son? Her son who knew she was spying on him? I shiver. There's no way. Dimitri's fallen in with a bad crowd, but he'd never kill someone. Least of all his own mother.

But I still remember the screams of Anton, the pleading of the man as Dimitri and Slava's fists and boots worked him over.

"You're going to help me," he commands, his eyes narrowing as he continues to force me to look at him. "And we're going to find out who killed my mother. And then, I'm going to make him pay."

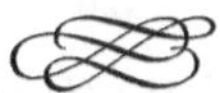

CHAPTER 11

"May her memory be eternal."

Dimitri gave a tight smile to the oft repeated phrase. The funeral had been delayed much longer than expected, and now that it's finally here, we both feel a bit... off.

Mourning someone who's been murdered is different than mourning someone who's died of natural causes, in that there's no way to really come to terms with how unexpected it is, and how much anger and hurt swirls within. I stand beside him as a chorus of well-wishers pass us by, dressed in black with somber expressions.

We still don't know who would've killed Rebecca, and the police are probably even further off the mark than we are. And now we're going through the funeral while her killer's still out there; mourning her loss while dealing with this simmering rage.

I look at Dimitri, and I wonder if he feels the same way as I did when my father was killed. If maybe now he's starting to understand why I clung to him so much, why I was so afraid that I'd die at any point in time. I was sixteen, torn between dealing with something most adults never have to deal with and just wanting to see my daddy again.

Sure, my dad fucked up with my mom in the end, but he didn't deserve to die like that, no more than Rebecca did.

"Their memory will be forever with us, in our hearts and prayers," another old woman says in a thick Russian accent, shaking both of Dimitri's hands at once. "Rebecca was a dear girl," she says, leaning in to whisper towards Dimitri in Russian. It's just the three of us near the coffin, the rest of the guests further away.

It's been years, but I still recognize that word she uses in her too-loud whisper. *Avtorityet.* Slava had said that, the night he and Dimitri beat Anton.

I look back to the coffin, to Rebecca looking stunning even in death. A ribbon lay upon her forehead, a tradition I didn't really understand but accepted as my own.

"Thank you, Aunt Vera," Dimitri says, leaning in and kissing her greying hair.

She looks to me and nods before going to the Rebecca, kissing upon the ribbon before gently placing the two flowers with the others.

I'm exhausted, and numb, but when Dimitri's hand encompasses mine, I get another jolt of energy and give him a gentle look of gratitude.

"How are you holding up?" I ask, my voice just above a whisper.

"When this is over, it will be easier," he replies, and I wonder if he means the grieving... or the revenge.

CHAPTER 12

J'm hoping Joanna is out when I finally get home, but no luck. She wanted to come to the funeral with me, but it would just feel weird. Especially since I told her about how I nearly hooked up with my boss. I can't have her learning he's my stepbrother after I told her that.

She gives me that soft, kind of confused smile that people do once they find out someone you know died. The cautious look that says they don't even really know how they're supposed to feel, let alone what they actually feel.

"How was it?" she asks, and I set my purse aside, taking off my black high heeled shoes.

"Sad," I say on an exhale. "A lot of her business colleagues came early in the day, then mostly just family and personal friends. The memorial dinner was…" Strange? I don't really know what to say. Rebecca had us do all the same things for my father's funeral, saying that it was customary, and I was too young and filled with grief to argue at the time.

It's almost nice to know that this is how she would've wanted it, though.

"I'm mostly exhausted."

Joanna nods, then points to the TV with the remote.

"Wanna do a romcom or something? Might take your mind off things."

I agree and quickly change into my pajamas, returning with a bowl of popcorn. It reminds me of when I was a girl, snuggled in between Rebecca and my dad, watching some dumb movie. She wasn't always a witch to me, especially not when dad was still alive.

Joanna hits play and she settles back in the chair, stealing some of my popcorn.

"So was your boss there?"

"Yea," I admit, but the last thing I want to talk about is Dimitri. If he wants revenge, I know he's going to get it, and I know what he's capable of. Hell, he was only nineteen when he kicked Anton's ass, so who knows what he's capable of now.

"Bet he looked good in his suit," Joanna says with a sly grin. She has no idea that my boss is Rebecca's son, so of course she'd be light about it. Especially with how much I railed on Rebecca since I moved in with Joanna.

But she's not wrong. I'd have to have been blind not to realize how good Dimitri looked in black, his dark eyes cold and somber. He's biding his time.

"He always wears suits in the office."

"Oh right. Most guys I work with you're lucky to get them in a button-down shirt."

I'm trying to catch what the actor just said, but I glance at Joanna for a second before turning back to the TV. "Not Dimitri. He's always formal."

Damn it, I missed a joke. The actress's nose scrunches up and she looks adorable. I wish I knew what he'd said.

The movie pauses, and I figure Joanna must've missed it too, but when I look at her, she's staring at me with utter confusion on her face.

"Wait, Dimitri?"

Oh shit.

"That Dimitri?" she continues, her voice growing a bit louder. My face must be burning red right now and telling her everything she needs to know about the situation. When I'd told her my boss kissed me, I'd purposefully left out his name, because I bitched about Rebecca and Dimitri to her more than a few times. It was practically a part time job for a while.

Damn it.

"Yea," I admit. What can I do, lie to her about it? Pretend like it's all coincidence?

She leans back in her chair, staring straight ahead, and I can't make heads or tails of her expression. How the hell would I respond if I found out that she was working for her step-brother, went over to his place in the middle of the night and made out with him?

I put the popcorn to the side, folding my legs under me.

"And he kissed you?"

I nod.

My stomach is tightening into knots. I never told anyone else about Dimitri, about my feelings for him. Everyone would know how wrong it is, and how stupid I was for fooling around with him only to get burned. But I told Joanna all about the cold shoulder he gave me and how much he hurt me.

"What about before?"

I chew on my lower lip. "We were just kids," I say with a shrug.

"You were eighteen and he was, what, twenty?"

"Twenty-one."

"Not really kids, Sarah."

"I know," I admit with a sigh. "But he seems different. And we've just been spending a lot of time together."

"Because you work for him now."

"Right. And it just... It just kind of happened."

"Was that the first time?"

I shake my head, and all at once, I almost just feel

relieved. Even though she looks so shocked, and I'm dreading what she's about to say, just telling someone is a weight off my shoulders. My eyes dip down.

"It's not like we're really related."

"You grew up together."

"Not entirely. And we were always more friends than anything..."

She shakes her head, grabbing for her drink and taking a sip.

"Do you want to again?" I tilt my head and she clarifies, "Kiss him."

"Yea," I mutter. "But now's not the time for that. I mean, he's just lost his mom..."

She stares at me like I just said the stupidest thing.

"What are you talking about? He's a guy, Sarah. Fuck, it'd probably help him to get his mind off of it for a while."

I can't believe what I'm hearing. Of all the reactions I anticipated, that wasn't even on the list. My nose crinkles and I nervously tuck some of my blonde hair behind my ear.

"Are you serious?" I mutter, and I imagine his lips pressing against mine, the taste of cinnamon burning my mouth as his tongue flicks against mine.

"Sure. I mean, if you're both into each other, why not?"

"I might get hurt."

"Well yea, Sarah, that's a relationship for you. I've been dumped by how many guys since you've known me? And dumped even more. It stings, but you move on."

"But then I wouldn't have him in my life anymore."

"You didn't have him in your life for two years and you survived," she reminds me, and I know she's right. But Dimitri hurt me so bad before, I just don't know if I can go through that again. But the thought of it working out... That hadn't even really entered my mind.

I nab another piece of popcorn, tossing it in my mouth and chewing it slowly.

"Just show up to his house?"

"That's what you did last time, right?"

"Yea."

"And he didn't leave you again when you left without putting out?"

I laugh, my nose crinkled in distaste.

"Well, no. I had to keep seeing him at work. Though..."

Now I have her full attention. Joanna turns and looks at me curiously.

"Well, it's just... before we got the call, we were in my office and..."

"And... oh my God, you were making out in your office?"

My cheeks are burning with embarrassment. I've never really had another girlfriend to talk about sex stuff with. Not that there had been any sex stuff to tell before now. I've been too busy focusing on just staying above level to date, not that I had a lot of interest in it anyways.

"Holy fuck. You guys screwed?"

I sputter, shaking my head, my face hidden from her.

"We... No. I mean, almost, but then the call came..."

"Awkward," she said with a half-smile. "Talk about a massive cock-block."

I throw a pillow at her, hitting her in the side of her head, "Joanna! Your mouth is getting filthier by the minute."

She throws it back at me, threatening to knock over my popcorn before I catch it just in time.

"Yea, well, you're the one screwing your step-bro, so I'm hardly the dirtiest one here," she teases back, her words so light and lacking in judgement. It's a relief to talk about it, to hear it said so plainly, and I lick my lower lip, drawing it into my mouth.

"So you think he'd like if I just dropped over?"

"Hell yea. Damn, if my mom died, I'd be desperate for a distraction. Especially if I were a guy. It's not easy dealing with that, especially by yourself, you know?"

I nod, taking a deep breath.

"You don't mind if I go?"

She rolls her eyes.

"Get out of here. You don't need my permission to sleep with him. Just be careful."

CHAPTER 13

I know that if I show up again and don't go through with it that things are going to get bad between us. Especially now that he knows that Rebecca was spying on him and I was helping her. I have no idea how much he knows about it, but it seems like more than enough to be justifiably upset.

I sit on the subway, watching the lights of the city flicker past, anxiety swirling in my stomach. It doesn't help that Joanna lent me this sexy black dress that I feel like I have no business in. I know I look pretty good in it, and it shows off my cleavage, but it still somehow feels weird.

No, what feels weird is that you're going to your stepbrother's house in the middle of the night to try to seduce him. Again.

I try to shake off the thought but I know that's at

the core of what's bugging me. But I can't get the thought of his body out of my mind. The way his mouth burned into mine, the hickey he gave me that I had to covertly hide for the funeral. It's like it's all out of some strange nightmare, yet I can't wake up.

I don't want to. Not before I know what he feels like, covering my body.

The memory sends a jolt through my spine and when we finally get to the stop near his place, I practically sprint off the train. My high heels make my strides shorter, my legs longer and shapelier, and I tug my jacket around me a bit tighter. I know what I'm wearing beneath it is scandalous, but the people of Brooklyn don't need to know that.

The beautiful exterior of his condo looms over me and I push in. This time I'm expecting the security guard, and my back straightens, my chin lifted just a little.

"Sarah Fairfax for room 1510, please. Mr. Brokov."

The security guard nods, calls up, and hesitates on the phone. What's Dimitri saying? If he's refusing me entry, I would be so humiliated, and some of my confidence leaves me.

The security guard covers the receiver with his palm and I move closer.

"Mr. Brokov wants to know if this is about his Uncle."

That jerk. I flush, my heart pounding faster in my

chest at the reminder of our safeword, of what I'd said last time when I'd run off, away from him.

"No," I mutter. I wanted to sound more suave, more in control, but as always, Dimitri keeps me off guard and always has the upper hand.

"Yes, Sir," the security guard says before hanging up the phone. "Come with me, Ms. Fairfax," he says, moving towards the elevators. At least Dimitri's letting me up.

Though now I'm almost positive I shouldn't be here.

The fifteen floors pass even slower than they did last time, and by the time I enter the beautifully decorated hallway, I feel faint from the blood rushing from my brain. Every time he torments me and I simply get more and more turned on. I have to feel him. I have to just let go.

One night of pleasure, of letting myself experience something I've wanted for so long.

The walk to his door is excruciating, especially when I open the door and see his wicked grin. He's wearing a shirt and jeans, so I guess he hasn't been to bed yet.

I swat his shoulder. "Jackass," I murmur, and he locks the door behind me.

"You love it," he says, leading me in and pausing at the bar before thinking better of it. "Can't sleep?"

I shake my head, my coat still wrapped tightly around my torso. Though when I see his eyes trail down my body, lingering on my calves, I know he's confused.

"Going to a bar or something?"

"Not that I could even if I wanted to."

He rolls his eyes. "Girls a lot younger than twenty get into clubs here, Sarah."

"Oh, right." Of course they do. Other girls who are refined and sexy and confident enough to flirt their way in. Not girls like me.

He leans against the bar, staring at me, waiting for me to explain why I'm here but I don't really have words. I thought it'd go differently, like we'd just pick up from where we left off, but that was over a week ago, and so much has happened since then.

I step towards him, my hands trembling as I slowly let the coat fall open, revealing the black dress beneath. I felt so sexy getting into it, but now I'm just a shy, self-conscious mess.

"You said, last time, that... bad things happen if you have a booty call and don't..." I trail off. I sound so stupid, like a kid pretending she's a seductress.

Though when my gaze meets his, his eyes are filled with fire and temptation.

He pushes himself from the bar, licking along his lower lip. He stalks towards me, and the warmth from his grin has warped into something much more dangerous.

"Is that what you want?"

My heart races. My lower lip quivers.

I nod, and heat boils in my veins as his mouth crushes against mine. There's no sweetness, no exploration, just a hunger unlike anything I've ever experienced before. Not from him, not from myself. When our bodies meet, it's with a fury that's been contained for years.

He lifts me, hands gripping my ass as he takes me to his room, tossing me onto the bed like I weigh nothing. His breathing is hard as he stares down at me before he tugs up his t-shirt over his head, unveiling his muscles and tattoos once more.

The light is dim, but my eyes still race excitedly over them as his hands next go to work on his belt. The jangle of metal and leather fill the air as he steps towards me.

"You're not getting away this time," he swears, and I'm filled with a sense of dread and desire.

He's dangerous. I know that better than most. That fire in his eyes is going to burn us both before long, but I don't care. Not now.

He grabs for my waist over my coat, and I lean in to kiss him, but instead he steals the fabric belt from my jacket. I blink, surprised, but his hand is on my knee, caressing it, and I relax into his touch.

"I'm not going to let you run. You want this too fucking bad for me to believe you when you say that escape is what you want."

He wraps the belt around his hand before tying it around my bare ankle.

"Are you wearing panties?" he asks, and I can't even respond.

I'm breathing too fast, too hard, and I'm trying to remain sensible but it's no use. I'm a slave to my needs, and I shake my head no.

That earns a feral growl and a brief glance up my thighs, as if he could see even though they're still pressed together so tightly. He yanks them apart harshly, tying my right leg to the solid wood of the bed post.

"You're not getting away," he promises, and when I feel that first press of his mouth against the inner side of my knee, I can't imagine why I'd want to be anywhere else.

His mouth is so warm, and it's traveling up, his light stubble tickling along my sensitive inner thigh.

It's not what I expected when I came over, but as his mouth gets nearer and nearer my pussy, I'm filled with an electric shock that trails through all of my nerve endings. His tongue teases out, tasting my thigh as his eyes watch me all the while.

I'm so warm, my heart pounding so fast and my breathing so hard that I'm nearly hyperventilating. But when his mouth finally grazes against my sex, it's like the entire world just stops. My breathing, my racing thoughts, my fears and inhibitions are all drowned out by the immense pleasure at having his mouth against me.

I moan, and his hard hand pins my thigh back, lifting my calf up over his shoulder. My dress is rolled up around my hips, my jacket half off, my blonde hair fanned beneath my arched head.

"Dimitri," I whisper, and he pushes in harder, his tongue caressing along the seam of my pussy, tasting me. Maybe I should be embarrassed or afraid, but I'm not. Instead, it's almost like relief washing through me. Relief that the world didn't end just because I want this more than anything and am finally getting it.

My fist wraps around the soft blankets, holding onto it as he starts licking me more hungrily, a growl passing through his mouth and into my sensitive flesh. I'm already so embarrassingly wet but he seems to love it, his entire body moving as he eats me out.

My skin prickles with excitement, warmth flooding me as his tongue lashes against my clit and then retreats, teasing me to higher and higher points of ecstasy with each motion. His mouth is delicious, and my head rocks back.

"Ah," I gasp, his hands grabbing my hips and pulling me closer to him. He doesn't let up, even though I'm already squirming like crazy, the sensations building so fast that I can barely do anything more than pant and writhe. He growls and I try to calm down, but I can't. He's just too good, feels too good, and I'm too sensitive for it.

And then he pulls away, just slightly, and I'm left at the peak of no return, anger and desire making my blood boil hotter. I'm like a volcano about to erupt and it's not comfortable being so close to the peak with no release.

"Dimitri?"

His grin told me that I was going to love and hate the next words out of his mouth. His lower jaw shone with my juices, and I feel like I should be embarrassed but I'm not. I'm more curious about what he'll feel like inside me.

His hand moves, the rough pad finding my clit, rubbing against the wetness there as he looks at me.

"I'm not going to make you come and let you leave again, Sarah," he says.

I tug my leg, the one that's bound to his bed, and it makes a little springy sound. "I can't run," I remind him.

His free hand goes to his jeans button, pushing it through as he simply presses against my clit with his thumb. He's not moving, not teasing me, not bringing me any closer to release. Just keeping me on the edge.

"I don't want to risk it," he says, and then he takes out his cock and everything he's said in the seconds prior is momentarily forgotten.

I don't want to be crass, I really don't, but I love

his cock. Ever since I first glanced a peek at him changing I've been dreaming of it. Of what it'd feel like.

He strokes it, watching me as I stare at it, and his grin widens.

"You've always been too afraid to lose it to this dick, haven't you?" he growls, and when I nod, he rubs my pussy a little bit more. Stoking those fires just a bit higher.

"You've wanted it for so fucking long. And tonight, you're finally going to get it. And I'm not going to let you go until I show you what I can really do."

My eyelashes flutter and I moan in spite of myself, my nipples stiffening against the dress to the point that they almost hurt. He strokes himself and my pussy in unison, teasing me. He wants me begging for it, but my mind is mush.

Grasping his cock at the base, he smacks his dick against my slit, and I'm so lewdly aroused it makes a crass wet sound. The grin on his face says he's enjoying himself, but he doesn't let up on his teasing. His attempts to make me cave to him.

"You've played with fire too long," he taunts me, still circling his thumb about my clit, bringing me to the edge of oblivion but always, always, pulling back before I find my bliss.

I want it — him — so bad, but it still feels wrong. Every young woman thinks about how she's going to lose her virginity, and I'm way out of my depths with him.

So why does that excite me so much? Why does his crassness make me squirm rather than making me want to run? I've ran every other time, but now it feels right in a weird way. Like the stars have aligned. Or maybe it's just that with me tied to the bed I feel without options. That to call it all off from here would be too much, too hard.

My eyes roll back and I want to curse him out, but instead I reach out, trying to brush my fingers against his stiffness.

I catch a brief touch of that thick pillar of his, the molten steel of his manhood against my fingertips. It's smooth and ribbed with his bulging veins, and oh so hot to the touch, but it's a fleeting moment, because Dimitri brushes me off immediately.

"*Nyet,*" he says, his voice husky, low and taunting. "Not for you," and I can hear the accent rising out in his words as he replaces his teasing thumb with the thick, purple tip of his cock. "Not unless you beg," he adds, looking at me with a devilish light in his eyes.

And for a moment he's of two worlds right before me. To look at him, I see the man I've crushed on for years, teasing and grinning. But that wickedness and authority in his grin and gaze reminds me of the darkness within.

Of the desires I've tried to forget I even have. The

ones that wake me in the dark of night, panting and longing for him with such depravity.

I bite down on my lower lip. I can't beg. The very thought makes my skin warm and I can tell I'm blushing as the butterflies in my stomach pick up their tempo. I haven't thought this through very well; I know that, but my desperate need for him...

I've been teasing myself just as much as I've been teasing him, and maybe it's a lapse in sanity as I open my mouth and the softest, "Please," I've ever spoken comes out from between my lips.

The slow circles of his thick, dark crown continue unabated, teasing me so masterfully as he watches me, soaks me all in.

"Please what?" he asks me, his voice so dark and ominous, so dangerous. And I know he's not going to be satisfied with something quite so meek as that. He has me trapped, under his control, and he's not going to stop so easily.

And both seeing and hearing him sound so dangerous... it makes him all the harder to resist. My mind is hardly in any position to notice his own broad, muscular chest heaving with his elevated breathing, his excitement for me so high it did more to him than a vigorous workout.

I have to look away from him. The dark shadows make his eyes seem even darker, and his lips are twisted in enjoyment. He likes watching me squirm, and I know it.

If I'm being honest, part of me likes how he makes me squirm. How I know this is wrong and yet I want it anyways. I swallow, and my voice is soft and wispy, contrasting against his intimidating growl.

"I want you, Dimitri," I manage, my breathing so much harder, the black dress feeling too tight around my chest. "I want to give it to you."

My words do a number on him, because Dimitri's feral eyes widen, and that devious glint becomes one of pure lust instead. The real proof came in the form of his cock.

He guides that thick, throbbing member down from my clit and forces it into my pussy. He's not a complete savage about it, but he splits my pink folds open around his shaft as he sinks on down into me.

He doesn't need to be mean about it for it to hurt though; it's my first time and he's oh so big. That thick shaft much harder to squeeze in then I had even imagined it would be.

The last thing I want is Dimitri thinking I'm a wimp, but I can't help the pained gasp that escapes me. He slows down, his head tilting, and for a second I wonder if he's waiting to see if I'll cry uncle but I don't. I can't.

Not now.

I bite down on my lower lip and nod at him, and he's slower this time and my juices help a little bit as he presses himself into me.

Dimitri gasps and moans, taking a grasp on my thighs as he edges himself into me, bit by bit, stopping now and then as my squirming takes over against my will. I can feel every throb of his arousal, and the way it stretches my pussy nearly beyond the point of bearing.

"Fuck Sarah," he says in a husky, breathless voice. "You weren't kiddin'... you really did save it all this time," he says, looking me over, as if even he didn't believe it. The man who could see through my every attempt to lie or mislead. "You're so fucking tight."

The fact that I made him drop his arrogance for just a few seconds thrills me, and I shift to get into a better position. My legs are spread so obscenely wide it looks almost painful, and between them is him, all tattooed and hulking, pinning me against his body.

I shudder at the sight and my eyes roll up in my head. He looks like an Adonis. A tattooed Greek sculpture. I can barely believe my eyes, let alone the way his cock is making my mind swim.

He grasps my thigh with one hand, while the other rough, strong grasp makes its way up my body. He feels out my figure, over my dress, along my chest, squeezes my breasts as he edges into me a bit more, making us both moan.

"*Bozhe moi* Sarah," he curses in Russian before leaning down and aggressively kissing my lips, a hard, primal kiss where his tongue delves into my mouth while he nudges the last of his length into my depths with a final thrust.

My mind is foggy, and I'm so warm, so happy. After so long of waiting for this moment, it's even better than I could have ever anticipated. Every throb of his shaft sends a thrill through me, our breathing quickening as we push against each other.

He's so much stronger, though, and the back of my head presses hard into the bed as his muscled body overcomes me.

Those powerful fingers of his sink into my flesh, and he uses my body to brace himself as he tugs back his hips. That girth of his pulling my pink labia as he slides back, glistening with my honey.

The low, pleasured moan he gives fills the air, his gorgeously muscled body rippling with the effort. Right before he plunges back into me again.

It's a slow motion at first, but the next one comes a little faster, and for the first time in my life I'm having sex. Really doing it! And with the man of my dreams no less.

"You're finally all mine, Sarah," he growls out as I stare up at his tattooed form, seeing the beast beneath the suits and civility for what he is. "And you aren't getting away ever again," he insists before covering my mouth with his once more for another aggressive kiss.

He's everywhere. I can smell him, taste him, *feel* him. I kiss him back, opening my mouth a little and letting his tongue invade me, that wet muscle pressing in against mine. I moan, and lift my free leg to wrap around his body, holding him close.

He finds a rhythm, and after a few moments, the pain dims and in its wake is bliss.

It is no longer just the thrill of finally being with him, of losing that niggling little thing called my 'virginity', it feels good as he thrusts his hips and fills me to my utmost depths. The air is rife with the sound of his balls slapping against my ass, and he picks up pace, those fingers of his holding me with an iron grip as he squeezes my thigh and breast.

Dimitri lifts my leg up over his waist, and looks down at me through narrow slits as he arches his back. He's pounding into me deeply, savoring the way my body rocks with his hammering thrusts.

"You're all mine now," he growls out in that delightfully harsh accent that seems to thicken with his pleasure.

He looks so good, his body covered with a light sheen of sweat, making his muscles even more prominent. I stare, transfixed, my entire body screaming for something I don't have words for. I've been pent up for so long that these sensations are already bringing me close to my climax.

Every contour of his rippling abs is on display thanks to that light perspiration, and I can see him in intimate, glossy detail. The way his biceps bulge, his pecs twitch, but most perfectly… the way his manhood plunges down into my puffy slit, vanishing from sight only to slide back out a moment later.

It's all so dizzying, and he's slowly claimed by his own pleasure, his eyes shutting as he takes me harder. I can feel him tensing but then... then he does something I don't expect with him looking so lost in pleasure.

He reaches his thumb up from my thigh and presses upon my sensitive clit, prodding and circling it with such urgency as he barrels towards his own release.

"Come for me," he demands in a gravelly, grunting voice. "Come on my dick before I fill your pussy, Sarah."

I should be revolted by his crassness, but it sends a shiver through me that I can't believe. I know we're taking a risk, I know better than this, and I don't care. Not as those waves of pleasure crash down on me, making me tremble violently against his hard grasp.

The clench of my pussy brought him into pleasurable oblivion with me. He hammers into me again, and lets howl a deep cry. His cock thrusts into my depths, jarring me as he hilts himself. The thick spasms of his own climax rocking not only his shaft but his whole, glorious body as he pumps every spurt of his seed deep into me.

His final thrusts are erratic, but they are so strong and needful, and he looses every drop of his virile seed deep into my waiting womb. It is a care-less risk, but one I can't care less for at this moment. I just want to be one with him, to feel it all and appreciate how we've become one so completely, without obstacle or interference.

My arms wrap around him, clinging to him like I'm afraid he'll disappear now that it's done. I'm scared that he'll abandon me again, that this'll be the end of it, and yet the climax dulls my fears and leaves in its wake a sense of neediness.

"Dimitri," I murmur, and his mouth silences me.

His hands are all over me again, sliding up and down my sides, feeling out every inch of my figure. He feels as hungry for me as he did before we even started, and he squeezes me in those powerful arms, kissing me so deep it steals all my words, then my thoughts.

The two of us still laying there, intertwined, with arms, legs and loins entangled, and this time neither of us is in a rush to end it.

CHAPTER 14

I wake up in his arms, the blankets twisted around my legs. His arm weighs me down, slung along my stomach, and when I look over through bleary eyes, I see his still slumbering face.

His brows are knit, and he yanks me closer, as if fighting my stirring and not wanting to wake. I shimmy in nearer, staring up at the ceiling. My limbs ache, and my heart is racing, but I've never slept better in my life in all honesty. Held in his arms, his hot body held against mine, it was bliss and I didn't want to escape it so soon either.

"Mmm," he growls, his dark lashes parting to reveal his cocoa colored eyes. "Sarah." His lips pull into a smile and then he lunges at me, and all of the peace of the morning is shattered by our cries of pleasure.

* * *

BACON, eggs, toast, and freshly squeezed orange juice. It's funny how just a simple meal can bring back so much nostalgia, and I look at Dimitri with a crooked smile. He gave me one of his button down shirts to wear, but it's way too big for me, and I have to pull up the sleeves to grab my fork.

"Just like dad used to make," I say, and I'm not sure if he made it especially for me or if he just liked the tradition of it. From his grin, I know I'm not getting an answer.

He slathers some jam on his toast, crunching on it as he stares across the table at me.

"I decided our next move," he says, and I tilt my head. For a second I don't know what he's talking about. Rebecca's death is the last thing I want to think about, but investigating who killed her is a dual edged sword. *'Curiosity killed the cat,'* keeps ringing in my head.

"Oh?" I stare back at him, uneasy. It's one thing to sleep with him, to have him absolutely punish my delicate body, but this is something totally different. Trying to act like everything's normal after doing it? Like it didn't affect him?

I'm kind of hurt, and take a sip of my orange juice to hide my frown.

"*Da*, there's a charity auction mother was to attend this Friday. She was to rub shoulders with some of the most powerful men and women in the city. If her hit was because of her business moves, then someone will have information there."

I just nod my head, not knowing what more to say. It's not like I don't want to find out. Hell, a part of me is excited at the prospect. I've always been far nosier than I should be, and finding out who exactly Rebecca pissed off? That sounds like icing on the cake.

"It won't be dangerous," he says, looking at me with those dark, smoldering eyes as if that's what I'm worried about. Honestly, the fact that it might be dangerous only made me more excited. What's wrong with me? "Just a bunch of rich twats who'll think you're there to pay your respects."

I narrow my eyes at him.

"You're not coming?"

He shakes his head.

"I have my own ways of getting information."

The room falls uncomfortably silent. I know his ways of getting information, and those are dangerous. As dangerous as it gets.

I lick my lips. Do I tell him I know about Anton? About Slava? I quickly decide against it. After all, it could just make him angry.

I cross my legs as I take another bite of toast, staring off in thought. The world goes fuzzy and I picture him in his car, driving to some seedy restaurant, his fist connecting with the face of the owner as he interrogates him.

He waves his hand in front of my face, snapping me out of my violent reverie.

"What's wrong?"

What's wrong? The fact that he's acting like nothing happened, like he and I didn't make love, that we didn't have a connection. The fact that he's just talking to me like I'm his *sister* who's helping him solve a murder case.

And then I feel his hand on my knee, groping up the bare flesh, and a shiver of calm goes through me. My eyes flutter and my shoulders relax. When I open my eyes again, he's grinning.

"I didn't figure you'd still be so pent up. Aren't you sore?" His lip quirks, his eyes so dark and dangerous that I can't look away.

"Yea," I answer honestly, but the idea of more sends a thrill through me that I can't deny. Just having his warm hand on my body is enough to send the butterflies in my stomach to fluttering and I lose my appetite.

He squeezes my leg, caressing it with his thumb as his expression softens for the briefest moment.

"I didn't want to overdo it."

And with that, all my worries about what happened simply fade into the background, and I smile at him earnestly.

But deep down, I know I can't go to a boring

charity dinner. No one there will confess to me that they killed Rebecca, of course, and any lead I did get would be smoke and mirrors. A woman like Rebecca pisses people off, and I'm sure that high society will be looking to point the finger at anyone they had a *bad feeling* about.

The night would be spent listening to people tell me that they think so-and-so killed her because they say Rebecca fired her, or what have you.

I have a feeling this goes a little deeper into a side of her I rarely saw. She hid it so well with her fancy clothes and her fake smile, but she married my dad before my mom's body was even cold. She'd been working him over like a professional, but I'd let it go out of respect for him.

So what I'm wondering now is: who she was trying to work before she died?

"Earth to Sarah," Dimitri says, squeezing my knee again. "Where'd you go off to?"

"Nowhere. Was just thinking about what I'll wear to the charity thing."

"Here," he says, moving to the bartop and grabbing his wallet, opening it up and handing me a black credit card. "Get what you want. Something to make you fit in. Look extravagant and appropriately in mourning."

"So... black."

"*Da.* Black. Go to Manhattan, to Bergdorf

Goodman and ask for Natasha. She knows me and will help you find something suitable."

I put the card in the breast pocket of the shirt I stole from him, nodding.

"Sure. Uh, pricewise?"

He raises his brow before just laughing.

"Nothing you can buy will put a dent in that," he says with a wave of his hand before returning to his breakfast.

"Dimitri," I start in protest. I've been poor long enough that it makes me uncomfortable to not have a spend limit. When I lived with dad, he spoiled me, sure, but I was too young to know any different. My needs have changed since then, and a no-limit credit card wasn't high on my list of priorities.

"Sarah, do this thing. Get some nice dresses. Not just for the event, but for dinners. I want to take you out. Show you off."

And he can't show me off as I already am?

He must be able to see the discomfort still on my face, because he strokes my leg again.

"Mother took from you all your father would've wanted you to have. It's time to get some of that back. Time for me to start righting the wrongs I turned a blind eye towards, or even worse, the hurt I gave you."

I lick my lips and let out a sigh. I don't know what I'm going to do about this new shopping trip, but my mind is already on something else. How I'm

going to follow him and find out who he's inter-
rogating.

I know he doesn't want me there because he's
trying to protect me, but I don't need protection
anymore. I already know what he's done and who he
is, and I haven't run scared.

"Don't you dare try to come up with a way not to
spend that money, Sarah," Dimitri scolds. "If I don't
see an offensively large number on my statement,
I'm going to drag you down there myself."

I roll my eyes, but don't put up a fight, and he
immediately knows that my mind is elsewhere.

"I promise, Sarah, it's not dangerous at all. Just
talk to mom's associates, see if there was anyone
holding a grudge or seems to be happy at her
absence. We'll take it from there."

"While you're doing your own interrogation?"

He stares for a few heartbeats before he nods.

"*Da*. Yes. While I do my own interrogation."

"Where?"

His jaw clenches for a second before he pushes
himself up from the table.

"That's not for you to worry about."

"But you want my help, Dimitri. You're gonna
have to play straight with me."

His eyes sparkle with mischievousness before
that quickly fades away.

"Just trust me on this, babe. You gotta stay away
from what I'm gonna do."

"Well you already came up with busy work for me, so of course I will."

He throws his hands up in the air and for a second I think he's going to snap. There's that brief flicker of anger that turns his mouth into a sneer and his gaze like daggers, and then he looks at me and it fades.

"Of course you will. But it's not just busy work."

"You asked for my help, Dimitri, to find Rebecca's killer. But now it seems you know something you're not telling me that's taking you in a direction you don't want me to follow."

He takes in a deep breath, and when he speaks, his Russian accent is even thicker with his anger.

"Sarah, you will do this thing I asked of you, and you will tell me all you learned. From there, we'll decide our next move. Together."

I know better than to argue with him now, and even as I nod, I'm thinking of ways I can find out where he's going. I remember his words from the last time I followed him, that *they* would have killed me before I even had a chance to regret spying.

I remember how angry he was when I lied to him.

And yet here I am, planning on doing it again.

CHAPTER 15

I don't get to Manhattan much anymore, and I like to keep it that way. Ever since I lost everything I had, I've hated seeing all those people going in and out of the high end stores as if it were just something they casually did for fun.

Walking out with bags and bags of clothes that cost more than my yearly rent? Yes, it makes me jealous.

So when I get off the subway at 57th Street, I'm already feeling a little uncomfortable. Dimitri acts like this is the easiest thing in the world, just walking into a store and having a personal shopper pick out lavish outfits for me, but this isn't a part of my life anymore.

And, unlike Carolyn from that TV show, I don't really long to go back to that world of high society.

The buildings tower around me, juice and cigars

and espresso bars lining the streets, each giving off a fragrant aroma that mingle with the smell of car exhaust.

I match the quick pace of the other pedestrians, staring straight ahead, lost in thought. What have I gotten myself into? It's one thing to try to work and earn this money, but just having Dimitri give it to me like this is cheap.

But it's not like he's just my step-brother any more. That ship has sailed, I guess. We don't even have any parents left binding us together, and after last night...

What does that make us? Lovers?

Or just steps with benefits?

It's not like I haven't wanted and dreamed of it for a long time. Even before our ill-fated attempt when I was eighteen, I was spying on him and crushing on him hard. Snapping pictures of him in the buff when I really, really shouldn't have.

And now what am I thinking? When he's stealing from his own company and involved with Slava again? I know he's dangerous as hell, so why am I so attracted to him, and willing to spend his ill-gotten cash?

Because he told you to, and you don't say 'no' to a man like that.

But I've said no to him twice, and he's respected it both times.

I'm shaken from my reverie by a tall, broad

shouldered man passing by me too close, knocking my arm. I latch onto my purse, fear jolting through me, and I glance over my shoulder but the sun is in my eyes and I can't make him out.

At least he never stole my purse.

I quickly slink into Bergdorf Goodman, smiling at the greeter before heading down to the beauty floor. It's a guilty pleasure still, and I can't afford any of my old favorites that dad used to get me. If I'm going to treat myself, it's going to start here, without a personal shopper looming.

The sales associate glances at me, giving me a smile before veering off to help someone else and I let out a sigh of relief. The music, the gorgeous decorations, the atmosphere... it's all so familiar and strange to me at the same time. Like I'm an intruder on a world that isn't mine anymore.

Opium perfume hides behind one of the glass cases, and instantly I can smell it, brought back to my thirteenth birthday and the beautiful gifts from my dad. Among the presents was that perfume. As he said it, I was now a lady and should smell like one.

I smile, the memory bittersweet, and inhale deeply before heading towards the nearest sales associate.

"Hey, I'm looking for Natasha?"

The curly hair brunette smiles the biggest smile I'd ever seen, offering out her hand.

"You found her! Who do I have the pleasure of meeting?"

She's so formal, but chipper at the same time, and instantly I'm set at ease.

"Sarah. Hey. My br—" *Don't introduce him as your brother, Sarah,* I chide myself. "Dimitri Brokov recommended you to me, said you could help me find a few things?"

Her eyes light up, dimples appearing in her cheeks.

"Of course! Where are we starting? The perfume you were eyeing?"

I flush, having not realized I was being watched, but I nod anyways.

"To start, yea. My dad... that was my first perfume. I haven't worn it in a while."

"Well I'm sure it'd be like putting on an old glove," she says before retrieving it, along with about a dozen samples. "Anything else? You'd look amazing in *Femme Rouge Velvet Creme Lipstick.*"

I look at the color, and even though red is not my usual, I give her a nod. If Dimitri wants to see his money drained, it's definitely going to happen with Natasha at my side. "And I guess, like, a smoky eye set? I don't really have a lot of makeup at home other than eyeliner and mascara, and both are running dry."

A few minutes later, and I have enough makeup

to last me years, and she's guiding me up towards the gowns.

"It has to be really nice," I say. "Black, something... I mean, it can't be scandalous."

She giggles, and sizes me up. "Sure, hun. I can definitely work with the sleek and elegant look. Especially with those red lips and that platinum hair. Black will be really striking against your milky skin too. What size are you? 4?"

Oh, she's good.

"Yea."

"And about... 5'4"?"

"5'3"."

"Okay, we'll likely need to hem it up a little, but that's fine. Oh, did you want me to grab you some champagne? We might be here a while."

* * *

It's like having a sea of clothing just washing over me, held up to my chest and quickly discarded. It's not that they're not nice — they are — they're just not me.

Natasha, however, is being really sweet and not seeming annoyed with me in the slightest, which is a relief. I take another sip of the champagne as she flicks through another rack of designer dresses.

"So how long have you known Dimitri?" she asks, giving me a look that tells me she knows, well... She knows he sent me to get some fancy and expensive clothes, so I must be someone of note.

"A few years." I don't really want to get into this. I've been trying to remain blissfully unthinking about the fact that we just slept together and I have no idea what that means.

"Oh? He started coming in here a year or two ago, and he's always been exceptionally generous."

"Is that so?"

"Sure. Always knows what he wants, but always makes sure to grab me so I can get my commission. I helped him the first time he came in and since then he's always taken care of me. Between you and I, he's the reason why management likes me so much."

I smile, but inwardly I'm shocked at how much he must spend here to make such an impact, especially with all the other celebs and famous families who shop here.

"What's he like with you?" I blurt out before I can stop myself. Why did I say that?

"With me? Oh, there's nothing funny going on, if that's what you're asking," she says with a giggle as she gathers a couple of black dresses and brings them over to me. "Always the perfect gentleman."

"Has he brought another woman here?" Okay, now I know I've had too much champagne. Do I even want to know?

Though the fact that she doesn't hesitate does buoy my spirits.

"Not even once. I was surprised to hear he was the one to send you. He always comes, gets his suits, then takes off. Not a big talker, but really charming. I was starting to think, well, you know…"

I quirk a brow, and she shakes her head, holding up one of the black dresses towards me.

"What about this one?"

I glance over it, and aside from the ruffles at the high neck, it looks like a normal, black dress to me. I shrug, and she puts aside the other ones.

"This one would look great, I think. Very formal and yet really fun at the same time. *Alexander McQueen*, so you know it's good quality and will last you forever, and with the slit up the thigh, it's not too stuffy."

It looks nice enough, so I smile at her.

"Sure, I'll try it on," I say, though honestly, I'm just so exhausted and want to find *something* suitable. Anything. I don't even know how I'm going to manage the energy to shop for more casual clothes after all this.

The dressing room we're in is, well, massive. Not like those claustrophobic things at the department stores. This one reminds me of a powder room Rebecca would have. A whole lot of space to move and breath.

I move behind the divider as Natasha opens the glass and lifts the receiver of the black telephone, ordering another glass of champagne. She must be able to tell I'm flagging, and probably a lot less excited than a woman with a man buying her an expensive gown should be.

It's not that I'm not grateful, I just don't know that I belong in this world anymore. But this is Dimitri's world.

So maybe it's really him I'm uncertain on.

I zip up the back of the dress, and look in the lit up three-way mirror, and suddenly all my fears have disappeared. I'm not a vain person, but I actually look really amazing in this! It's sleeveless, and with a high collar with ruffled material along my throat, giving it a regal kind of look. It nips in at my waist, and the slit in the skirt comes up to my thigh.

It's just the right mix of sexy and classic, just like Natasha had promised. She comes alongside and beams at me.

"Oh my God. I know just the shoes for that, too. With the red lipstick and... Will you be wearing a bracelet? You'd probably want something simple, diamonds or something," she says as she moves behind me, hands brazenly on my hips as she soothes out a crease. "And what did I tell you about your silhouette, huh? Makes you look like a nymph!"

I laugh, and just simply nod along with her barrage of suggestions. If she can pick out this dress, I'm sure she can finish the look off.

"Dimitri won't be able to keep his hands off you,"

she promises, and I damn the perfect lighting in here because it makes my blush even more transparent.

"We'll see," I say, sidestepping the fact that I don't even know if he's going to see me in it.

Natasha scurries off and a few moments' later returns with a pair of the most elegant shoes I've ever seen. They look more like jewelry than they do high heels.

In her other hand is another glass of champagne, which I once again eagerly accept.

"Those are beautiful," I say, and already I feel bad. This stuff is going to cost a fortune, but now I really want it. I make my way to the zebra striped ottoman, sitting down on it as she helps me on with the shoes.

"These are *Manolo Blahnik*," she says, and I remember the label well. "It's a crystal front and buckle, and with the light padding inside, it should help you stay on your feet all night, even with the four inch heel."

I stand up and, even though I'm not used to stilettos anymore, they are actually really comfortable. And damn, they look great with this dress.

"Aren't they gorgeous? That man is a *God* when it comes to ladies shoes."

"They're amazing," I say back with real surprise. I was not expecting to find anything I liked, let alone loved. I look at my reflection in the mirror, and it's like seeing a different person. Someone older, more classy and refined. It's a reflection I can get used to.

"You look *to-die-for*," she says and usually I think it would be over the top if I didn't actually kind of agree.

"You really think Dimitri will like it?"

"Oh honey, have you seen yourself? You're gorgeous, and probably one of the sweetest customers I've served all year," she says, her voice going low and a bit more confidential despite the privacy of our room. "And seriously... stick with him. He has a good heart, I can tell. He doesn't love often, but he loves fully, to hear him talk of it."

I stare into my blue eyes and let myself feel excited at her words. Maybe what we have is something special after all.

"He also suggested... I get some more every day clothes," I say casually and her eyes light up with enthusiasm.

It's going to be a long afternoon.

CHAPTER 16

"Holy fuck, Sarah."

I look at Dimitri, suddenly feeling very self-conscious. I know the dress isn't my usual, but I still wasn't expecting to see that fire in his eyes.

I might be inexperienced, but Dimitri's desire was always something I could see. It's like we're connected in some primal way, and when he grabs my hip, primal is definitely the word.

"I don't fucking want a single soul looking at you in this. No one but me should have that damn right."

My heart races, especially when he grinds against my side and his growing erection presses into me. I'm all ready for the charity ball, but he's weakening the small bit of desire in me to go. Maybe we should just give in, forget our mission to find the murderer. Leave it to the cops and just lose ourselves in passion over and over again.

How bad would it be to hide from the world like that?

My eyes meet his, and I know he's thinking the same thing, and his mouth presses against mine instantly. He's ravenous, hard, and gripping me with all his impressive strength. There's no escaping, and I feel so delicate, but I like it.

I really like it.

It's funny how everything got so much more complicated, and so much simpler, the second we finally gave into our base instincts.

His hand reaches towards the slit in the dress, pulling it away from my thigh. He's exposing me, his fingers exploring between the softer, untouched flesh of my thighs, then probing inwards. He seeks out my feminine heat, and I gasp as he finds me pantiless.

He growls, his teeth nipping along my throat and up to my ear.

"This better be for me," he warns, his voice so dark it sends a shiver down my spine. *Why does it turn me on?*

"It is," I whisper truthfully, and he rewards me by roughly petting my throbbing clit.

"I claimed you first. If I ever find out another man touches you..." His index and middle finger press inside of me, and I moan in pleasure, "You'll be the last thing he ever fucking touches."

A shiver travels down my spine, and suddenly I

feel too hot, even though there's a chill from the air conditioner. The mixed signals make his touch even more intense, and my knees begin to quiver.

What am I doing? Why am I so lost to a man like Dimitri?

He nips my ear, hard, and I gasp in shock.

"Do you hear me, Sarah?" he asks, his fingers stilling deep within me, not allowing me any bit closer to my own pleasure. My mind is fogged with lust and desire, and I fumble with my words as he bites my ear again.

"Yes," I hiss.

"Yes, what, Sarah?"

"No one else will touch me."

"And why's that?"

I gulp, my heart hammering in my ribs, his breath washing over my jawline.

"Because I don't want them to."

"Because you're mine," he corrects, and then his mouth smothers mine again, his fingers working faster between my slickened petals. I can't believe we're doing this so brazenly, as if it weren't so damn wrong, but when he guides me to the bed, excitement swirls in my stomach rather than disgust.

The bed presses against the back of my calves, and he topples me over onto the plush sheets. His fingers withdraw and he looks down on me, a storm within his eyes. I don't know what he's thinking about, but I know the spark between us hasn't diminished at all since our first time.

If anything, it's ignited into a more fiery flame.

"You are so fucking gorgeous," he says as his gaze trails down over my body. I'm half clad, the long skirt pushed aside to expose my legs and sex, my torso still held snuggly in the expensive, black fabric. I'm worried about destroying the dress, but he doesn't seem to care at all.

As if having sex with me was way more important than the thousands of dollars of his money I just spent on this outfit.

"You're going to go to that party with the memory of me on top of you," he promises as his hand goes to his belt. It's almost a threat, how slowly he unwinds it, his tongue dabbing his lower lip thoughtfully. "I'm never going to let you go again, Sarah. Do you know what that means?"

I nod, even though I don't. I have a feeling I barely know this man at all. The depths of what he can do, the things he has done since I was kicked out...

He's the most dangerous man I know, the one man I shouldn't be with, but as he strips off his shirt, my eyes are immediately drawn to his hard, ribbed form. Beneath the litany of tattoos, and the slight sheen of perspiration, Dimitri is perfect.

And when he puts his weight on top of me, my

inner thighs parted by his strong hands, I'm lost to heaven.

"Pretty soon," he murmurs before biting my lower lip and tugging it outwards, "you're going to know what it really feels like for me to fuck you."

The lower side of his cock presses against my pussy, and mixed with his words, another erotic shock goes through me. I grind against him eagerly, my mind lost to passion as my hands squeeze his muscular biceps.

"Once all this shit is over with, I'm going to make you scream so loud we'll get the cops called on us. You'll beg," he marks the word with a kiss upon my cheek, "and cry," another kiss, lower, "and plead for more." Finally his mouth finds mine at the exact moment that he spears me, silencing my moan of delight.

He's so big, his entire body weight pressing down on me as he wastes no time in beginning to thrust. I'm already so turned on that it's made a lot easier, and when he brings his finger to my clit, I'm in heaven.

I've wanted him for so long, and it's even better than I could've ever fantasized about. Even better than my first time with him, if only because it doesn't hurt quite so much.

Instead of fretting about the anxieties of my first time, I get to enjoy it fully. I can watch his hard, corded muscle over me, working like a well-oiled metal machine, whose sole focus and purpose was to piston that gloriously large cock into me.

I'm splayed open by his passions, my knees pulled back wide, my soft, puffy petals sundered and stretched around his veiny, throbbing girth. I try to hold onto something, but the bed won't do as he picks up pace and everything is heaving and jumbled. So I do the only thing I can: I cling to him, let my fingernails dig into his shoulders.

"Still so damn tight," he growls out, as the sounds of his hard body pressing into my softer, more feminine form grow louder and louder with his rising tempo. I feel like I'm melting beneath him, every little thing he does making flesh and bone turn to warm, molten lust for him in return.

He kisses me hard upon the lips, and it feels so passionate, so loving. The perfect counterpoint to how our loins mingle in rampant, shameless fucking. The hammering of his cock, the circling of his finger at my sensitive clit.

His tongue dances with mine as sparks begin to grow within me. A tingle rises from my sex into my torso before spreading to my limbs, like every part of me is being awakened by his body.

Everything feels more intense; every rub of his body against mine, the feel of the fabric against my stomach and chest. He growls my name against my tongue as he spreads my legs wider, fucking me deeper than before. Each thrust makes me squeak a little, but it feels so damned good!

Dimitri works me so masterfully; better than I had thought a man would, after all the disappointing tales from women I know. About how their experiences with men were too short, too painful, too long and unsatisfying.

No, he brings me so close to the edge within so little time with the dual thrusting of his cock and the machinations of his devious fingers. But just as I feel that coiling fire rise up in me, he pulls his hand away. He leaves a wet trail along my hip until he grasps my ass beneath, letting his powerful fingers sink into that fleshy mound as he keeps me perched upon the edge. Agonizingly. Heavenly.

He spares a look down between us, to watch the sight of his shaft, gleaming with my honey, sliding back out of me, labia clinging to me, right before he thrusts it back inside me.

"I'm never letting you go now," he growls through his lust-filled breaths, licking at his lips so hungrily.

He tastes as amazing as he looks, and feels even better than that.

"I don't want to leave you," I practically purr back, and I mean it with every fiber of my being. I know he's into some dangerous stuff, and all of his promises of darkness to come excite me rather than turn me away. I long for more.

He rewards me for my devotion by making not only my whole body quake with his renewed lusts, but the bed as well. Each hammer blow of his dick into me making the expensive bed creak and shake despite its quality make. My body seems to reverberate with the blows he lands upon me. I can feel the force ripple out through me, across my chest. And greedy for it, he reaches behind me, unzipping my dress.

He treats the expensive fabric as if it's nothing more than a mild hindrance in his way of getting what he wants.

I don't have time or the inclination to stop him as he yanks it from around my arms, pulling it down to let my breasts spill out and jiggle before his very eyes.

"Gorgeous," he growls at me, ogling my chest before he grasps a hold of one fleshy mound tightly, letting his fingers sink into the supple flesh. "Such perfect tits…"

I arch my back into him, the garment now wrapped around my stomach, leaving me wholly exposed to his wandering hands. He squeezes gently at first, slowing his thrusting only enough to pay reverence to my chest before both his grip and his thrusting grow harsher.

I'm precariously on the edge of orgasm, and when his finger and thumb pinch and tease my stiffened nipple, I swear I'm about to come. But then he denies me again, leaving me panting and wanting for more as he takes my full tit into his hand and massages it.

Those tightly grasping hands of his, strong enough to break a man's neck, were put to use fondling my tits, and groping at my thighs and hips. He wasn't rutting at me like some horny man out to bust his load and be done with it. He was claiming my flesh, inch by inch, reveling in my body for all it was worth. And he capped it off with another rough kiss to my lips, thrusting his tongue into my mouth as his muscular body continued to piston into me.

"*Bozhe Moi!*" he curses in Russian as he lurches back up, our lips popping apart. A shudder runs through his hard, ripped body as he lets loose of my breast and takes hold of both my hips. "On your knees," he commands in a gravelly husk of a voice.

I obey.

Instinctively, I want to. Need to. Whether it's that thin layer of warning lacing his voice, or just the fact that every bit of my body is crying for more, I quickly reposition myself to his liking.

But when he presses into me again, he goes deeper than ever, I'm sent forward in my shock. He captures my hips, roughly tugging me back into place, and I dig my hands into the bed.

There is no escaping from his passions; he holds me in sway, that iron grip of his unbreakable. And now each new thrust of his hips means a loud slap of his hard body against my ass cheeks, making the flesh ripple with each new noisy smack.

"That's my girl," he growls approvingly, but to contradict his words, he cracks his palm against my ass cheek, a singular, loud impact that makes me gasp out, and then he follows it up with another.

It sends a jolt of pain through me, but the shiver that follows is anything but bad. Suddenly my nipples stiffen even more, the sensation almost uncomfortable as my legs spread and I take him in deeper.

I never could have imagined that his punishing me could feel so amazing.

Punishing? Is it still punishment when he just did it for the hell of it? As reward for me being good?

I'm not sure, but I'm getting light headed, clinging to the bedsheets as he takes control of me further, making me teeter upon my hands and knees. He's like a freight train, and though his hard body glistens with a thin sheen of perspiration over his hard, stony muscles, he's not tired, not even a little weary.

"It took too long for this," he rasps out, rubbing my stinging ass cheek so threateningly. "But you were worth the pain."

Every time he rams into me, an electric jolt sparks throughout me, and my body so desperately wants — needs — to come. It's cruel to keep me on the edge like this, and yet...

I love it. I love how in control he is, and even when he denies me that ultimate pleasure, the buildup, the tension, is like a drug I can't get enough of.

"Dimitri!"

His broad shoulders tense up, and all those gloriously toned muscles clench and bulge. He's fighting the pleasure now, I realize, trying to savor me a while longer. But I don't even know how much more I can stand!

"Sarah," he growls out between his grinding teeth, and I feel his dick swell within me, straining the walls of my tightly clenching pussy. He's a beast of a man, and those hands grasping my thighs still hold me in place, helping move me forward as his hips tug back, then pulling me in again as he thrusts forward.

"Oh God," I curse under my breath, my head swimming with all the sensations. He feels so amazing, and even without him touching my clit, I can feel that pleasure mounting, getting ready to send me over the edge.

Our bodies are working in unison, both of us so needy for release, for that ultimate form of bliss. Even knowing how close I am, though, doesn't prepare me for when it finally strikes me, fast and furious as he begins to pound into me as hard as he can.

I'm a writhing, twitching mess as he hammers

into me, but he lets loose such a lion's roar that it quakes the decorations upon the wall. He's a furious font as he ploughs in harder and fast, spurting his creamy seed as he strikes my ass cheek, makes me gasp out amid my own climax, then reaches in around to torture my over stimulated clit.

It's all so much — too much! — but he's driving us both to our limits as he pounds in, spurting stream after stream of creamy seed into me. Both of us being milked for every moment of pleasure, every droplet of thick come and every gush of warm honey.

The pleasure lingers forever and fades too fast, all at once, and I'm left a quivering, mewling mess. He thrusts into me a few more times, slower now, lazier, just drawing out the last of our bliss and sending another aftershock through me until he finally withdraws.

I pant for breath as he walks to the bathroom, returning a second later with a soothing, warm wash cloth. His face is flushed, his smile deadly, as he presses the cloth against my battered sex.

He cups my pussy, and the warm soothing cloth stems the flow of his creamy seed as it drools from my puffy slit. And in this moment, he's proving that while he can be a total prick, he cares about me. Even dotes on me.

"That was more like it," he says with a wry smile, leaning in and placing a tender kiss upon my temple, then gingerly brushing away the few stray strands of hair glued to my forehead with perspiration.

I smile as I relax, his tender touches easing me down from the earlier high. It's in this moment, when he looks at me with such affection, that I really start wondering if I've gotten in over my head.

Not because he's dangerous. Not because he's potentially in the Russian mafia.

It's because I might actually be totally and utterly in love with him.

CHAPTER 17

I'm not proud of what I did. I'm really not.

But I put a tracker on Dimitri's phone. He'll kill me if he finds out, I just know it, but I'm taking that risk because he insists on driving me to the charity ball. He's likely figured that I'd try to find some way around this, and he's right.

He leans in to kiss me as we sit in his car outside the manor. I'm expecting a chaste peck on the cheek, but instead I get intense passion, his mouth on mine, his hand cupping my cheek.

"Don't get in over your head, Sarah. Just relax, enjoy the night, and try to find some information we can make use of."

"I know. I'll be fine, Dimitri. No one's going to try anything at a charity event."

He looks towards the large building that looks

more like a museum than a home and gives his nod of approval.

"You're welcome to come back to my place, but I likely won't be home tonight," he says.

He must see that it rankles me, and his fingers caress the spot behind my ear that he found during one of our trysts.

"Don't worry. I've handled worse than what I will tonight. I promise," he says.

I nod, but I know that as soon as I go in there, say hello to a few people, and make an appearance, I'll have done my duty well enough to sneak off for the night. Especially if I can find someone to say something upsetting to me.

Not my proudest hour, but they never said it'd be easy trying to peek into the seedy underbelly of Brooklyn.

I don't know what he's planning, not really, but if he's going to be out all night, there's always going to be a risk of something really awful happening.

That's why I put the tracker on his phone. Not just so that I can spy, and try to find out what's really happening, but that I need to keep an eye on him. He told me before that if *they* knew I was spying, that I'd be killed without a second thought.

Yet I'm doing it again.

"Will you call me to let me know everything's okay?" I ask.

He shakes his head, though, and his dark eyes stare into mine.

"I won't have reception. And you need to not worry about me," he says.

"Tough luck there, Dimitri," I say with an exasperated sigh, getting out of the vehicle and slamming the door closed. Of course, the passenger side window is still rolled down from earlier, so lot of good that does me for having the last word in our argument.

"Just have fun tonight, Sarah. Loosen up, have some drinks, get a cab home safe," he says, and then his eyes drop down, over my fancy new outfit.

The one he'd defiled me in earlier.

"I wish I could come with you, show you off to all those pompous assholes," he says with a bit of lightness to his tone.

I roll my eyes, folding my arms beneath my chest.

"Nothing's stopping you, especially since you think someone in here might know who murdered your mother. That's why you've stuck me on this job, right? You figured I'd use my detective skills to schmooze with people I hated when my dad was still alive?"

"Sarah," he sighs, defeat weighing heavy on his shoulders. "Let's not get into this. Go. Once we are through this night, we will talk about..."

He trails off, and I can tell by his expression that I'm not getting anything more out of him.

"Fine, Dimitri. Go. Don't do anything stupid."

He grins at me, but drives off without making a promise. Not a good sign.

I sigh and turn towards the mansion. I hate this stuff, I always have. I know that the rich kids always have a bad rap of being spoiled, and maybe once upon a time I was, but being homeless and struggling?

That knocked me out of that real fast. I grew up more in those few days on the streets and the couple of years struggling just to eat than I care to think about, and I like who it made me. I'm harder now. Stronger. More independent.

Not independent enough that you refused Rebecca's offer for financial security, I chide myself.

And with that morose thought, I head into the party.

For all my misery in having to go to this event instead of where the real action was, I have to admit that walking into a party in thousands of dollars' worth of fine clothing is a boost to my ego. Not much of one, but at least I only feel out of place rather than looking out of place.

I smile pleasantly at the greeters before looking around at the large foyer ahead of me. Beautiful marble flooring and a staircase that likely cost more than the house I'm renting the basement of. Lights twinkle, the chandelier sending rainbows about the ceiling and floor.

It's still quiet, but I make my way into the ballroom. Classical music played by a live band soothes my ears, relaxing the tension in my shoulders as I slowly start to unwind. Going to an event without a friend or acquaintance is akin to torture, I'm certain.

But when Mr. O'Reilly touches my bare arm and his ruddy face lights up, I know this is even worse. He used to be a business partner of my father, one that my dad never fully trusted and was always certain he was skimming off the top.

Dad couldn't prove anything, but I trusted my dad's business instincts if nothing else.

"Sarah! I thought that was you. Oh my, it's been four... no, five years now, hasn't it? You were only sixteen then, I remember you had your party."

I smile tightly, looking down at the stubby, unpleasant man.

"Must be about that, then."

"You've grown, haven't you!"

I'm barely aware of the rest of the conversation as he drones on with niceties, and condolences for Rebecca's death. He's the drabbest, dullest person and when I spot Samantha out of the corner of my eyes, I'm only too excited to excuse myself and go towards her.

Sam is the daughter of one of Rebecca's friends, and while she and I never had a lot in common, she has the biggest mouth of anyone I knew.

Two birds, one stone.

"Sarah!" she says with a big, fake smile, her lanky arms wrapping around me as she pulls me into an embrace. "You look so much older with that hair, I barely recognized you! And you've put on a few pounds too, haven't you?" she asks as if that were the most normal of things to say.

My self-esteem now perched on a craggy cliff, I give her my best fake smile.

"You look great." Unfortunately, I mean it. She's always been supermodel material, and in her expensive gown, even more so.

"Thank you, thank you. Jerome, my personal trainer, is just a *God*, seriously. You should look him up. I mean, he is g-a-y, but who isn't these days?" She bats her impossibly long lashes, glancing towards the bar. I'm not sure if she's hunting for fresh meat or looking for someone she knows, and before I can ask, she picks up again.

"So I heard you were, like, totally kicked out a couple years ago, huh? That must've sucked, especially with Rebecca taking all of daddy's money. Though I guess since you're here, things were smoothed out before she died?"

She's talking about me being kicked out and Rebecca being dead like some people talk about the weather: completely indifferent small talk.

"Yea, I guess. She contacted me a few weeks ago."

"Oh, yea, you must be turning twenty-one soon, huh? Gotta make arrangements for that trust!" Her red mouth warps into an excited smile as she wiggles her fingers to someone behind me.

"Trust?"

"Duh, your trust fund. God, Rebecca was always complaining to my sister about that, about how she was looking for a way around paying out. I guess that's why she kicked you out, thinking maybe if you were estranged, she'd figure something out."

I can't believe what I'm hearing. Samantha's acting as if this is no big deal, but I had no idea my father had put aside any money for me.

"Did she ever say how much?"

"Oh, you know I don't like to gossip, Rebecca."

Her blue eyes sparkle and I know I'm losing her interest. She's already spotted someone else.

"Oh come on, I'm going to get it soon anyways. Why not spoil the surprise?" I say with a curve to my lips that I hope makes me look sly. Like we're in on a secret together.

Samantha giggles and I have her hooked.

"Oh well, when you put it like that, when your father died he was worth $1.1 billion. Didn't you ever google him? He was all over the lists. Since Rebecca's expanded her own enterprise, I'd say both you and your brother are in for quite a good time. Especially if those rumors about her connections are true."

I'm in shock. I knew my dad had a lot of money,

but I didn't figure it was that much. He'd always been fairly low profile about his earnings.

"Hello? Earth to Sarah."

I shake my head to clear me of the stupor.

"How's Dimitri anyways? Still yummy as always?"

"I gotta go." I turn instantly, and head for the door. I need some air.

"Wow, rude," Samantha mutters behind me, and I brush past Mr. O'Reilly on the way out.

The night air has a slight hint of fall in it, and I'm grateful for how it cleanses my lungs. I gulp it in, my head feeling light, my stomach clenched. I go over the conversation in my head, over and over.

Is that why Rebecca was offering me that money? Was she trying to buy me off? She offered me half a million dollars which was unbelievable, but if dad had left me a trust fund with more than that...

My mind goes back to the contract that Rebecca had me sign when I accepted the job. One of the lines was legalese, telling me I had no right to sue for any other money in the future. I hadn't thought anything of it at the time, but now?

I feel like I'm going to be sick.

But wait, what did Samantha say? The rumors of Rebecca's connections?

Did she mean... mob connections?

I whip my phone out of my purse, looking at the time. It's already after ten. I call up the app to track Dimitri. He said that there'd be no cell reception where he was going, but at least I'll get the place where he last had reception.

I call for a cab. I should go home and change, but the last hit on the cell tower was already half an hour ago. Whatever Dimitri had in mind, it is already in progress.

"Where ya headin'?" asked the cabby as I slide into the backseat.

"I need to make a quick stop at Pacific Street, then 35th Street and 2nd Ave., Brooklyn. I'll tip for your time."

"Sure, doll," he says, pulling out of the building and heading me towards my home. I know I'm running out of time, but I'll be no help to anyone without changing my outfit, and grabbing my camera.

And my gun.

CHAPTER 18

I get out at the intersection, paying the driver before looking down the dark street. Cars that look partially abandoned litter the area, bars on all of the windows. Suddenly I don't feel so confident, and I pull my black hoodie a little tighter around my head.

This is the area that Dimitri was last in, so he must be in one of these buildings.

But what one?

There's an alarm going off at the end of the road, the wailing of the car alarm echoing off the high buildings and adding to my uncertainty. Maybe I should just go home, and listen to Dimitri for once. Maybe I really don't want to be here, and see what it is my lover's doing in this shady place.

I suck in a deep breath of air, walking slowly and

looking for anything that might lead me to where Dimitri is.

I don't see his car, and I keep to the side of the buildings, trying not to draw any attention to myself, even as my heart pounds in my chest. I've gone from my biggest stress being filing season to stalking my brother.

It didn't even seem like a long fall.

No street lamps line the road, and I can barely make anything out. I slump against the wall, considering what to do next. I can't just barge into any of these buildings, looking for Dimitri. It's useless.

I make my way back towards the marine terminal and the flickering, yellow light, when the alarm behind me stops. I can suddenly hear my own steps on the sidewalk, but worse than that, I hear someone else's. I can't see them, even when I glance around, and my pace quickens.

Dimitri warned me they'd kill me if they found out I was spying before, and if they catch me here, in the middle of the night...

Panic grips my chest, and I'm practically running down the side street, but the heavier steps behind me quicken to match my pace. And then faster. He's not far behind me, those thick thuds getting closer and closer.

I nearly run into a platform, lifted off the ground by a couple of feet, used by trucks for unloading material. My fingers grip it, and I find, blissfully, it's not solid. I have no idea what's beneath it, but I duck under in a crouch, hoping to throw whoever else was in the alley off my scent.

I hold my breath as I hear the footsteps near me at a jog. My heart is pumping so loud I'm afraid it might draw attention, and I squeeze my eyes shut. I'm so near to the main road, to the lights of the marine terminal, but I'm still submerged in darkness within my little hiding space.

The footsteps pass me, and I let out a brief sigh of relief. But then, for just a split second, he turns and I get a glimpse of who it is. A face I've forever remembered, and longed to forget.

It's Anton. The same man my brother beat up all those years ago. The man that Dimitri threatened to do terrible things to after he snitched on Dimitri's boss.

My stomach sinks. If Anton's free... what does that mean for Dimitri?

He glances around, and I hold my breath again, tears stinging my eyes but I quickly squeeze them away. I don't have time to get emotional about it, not if Dimitri's in trouble. I wait and watch, my legs burning from my awkward squatting position but I'm too afraid to shift and draw attention to myself.

My hand goes to my purse, grabbing my gun lightly in my hand, just in case.

Thank God there's no need.

He continues walking, back into the inky darkness of the alleyway. I watch him until he's far enough away from me before I move from my hiding place. My legs feel so good stretched out after being so cramped, but I don't have time to enjoy the sensation. Instead, I follow Anton into the dark.

I'm quieter this time, now that I know someone else is here, and even though he looks over his shoulder a few times, he never spots me. Slowly, slowly I make my way towards the building he enters.

Several minutes pass before I feel comfortable enough to enter. I have no idea what's awaiting me on the other side. He might be standing guard just inside the building, gun at the ready, so I hold mine up to my chest.

If they have Dimitri, I'm going to have to do what it takes to get him back. Luckily, dad used to take me shooting and Rebecca insisted on self-defense classes, but that hardly makes me feel any bit more comfortable. It could be the end.

I beg myself to turn back, to just go back to Dimitri's condo and hope for the best, but I've always been stubborn and curious to a fault. My dad used to call me his little daredevil.

Kneeling, I touch the handle of the door, cautiously turning it. Every second feels like an eternity, but I have to go slow. Quick movements draw the eye and create more sound, two things that would definitely attract trouble. Staying down helps so that if they do shoot, they'd not be shooting down, hopefully.

I begin the tedious process of opening the door, and when I finally get inside, there's no one there. Simply a large room filled with crates.

I close the door behind me, moving in with cautious footsteps. Even though my blood is racing, my breathing is deep and calm. Keep cool under pressure. I have to keep cool.

But when I hear the unmistakable crack of fist on skull, I can't help but cringe as I picture Dimitri's gorgeous face taking a pounding.

I quicken my pace, rounding the nearest stack of boxes only to find a staircase leading down. The stairs are iron, and sure to echo, so I can't chance it. Instead, I get down on the flat of my belly, leaning in so that I can glance down from above. I'm in the dark, so I pray they can't see me as I peek out.

But what I see is not what I expect.

There stands Dimitri — his fist bloodied, his face fierce — looming over a man I don't recognize with dark hair and olive skin. Anton's at his side, wringing his hands, and a truck of a man stands to the side, watching over the proceedings.

Dimitri brings his fist to the bound man's face again, his eyes already swollen and his lip bust open.

"Who had Rebecca Fairfax killed?" he asks, his voice very clear and deliberate.

Anton then starts speaking in another language I

vaguely recognize as Italian, his voice quicker and more frenzied.

The man tied to the chair looks at Anton, replying back in the same language. They were using Anton as a translator? But he'd betrayed Dimitri. Was a snitch. Why would Dimitri trust him again?

"He says it wasn't the Italians!" Anton translates into English, but Dimitri clearly doesn't believe him.

"You said she was using our laundering scheme to get money to the Italians so that they could invest it for her without anyone being the wiser," Dimitri snarls.

"It's true! She was!"

"And you said that this guy is the money guy."

"He is!"

A few more brutally quick jabs of Dimitri's fists into the guy's torso, and he's coughing blood. Then the bound man starts speaking again, and Anton translates once more.

"He said he worked with your mother, that she owed him money, but he'd never kill her. She was always good for her loans. It'd be a bad business decision."

"Viktor," Dimitri says, and I recognize the name. That's the man who had arranged for Anton to be picked up by Dimitri and Slava. The one that was to be promoted.

"*Da?*"

"I need to talk to Anton in private. Take this

izhets," Dimitri spits the Russian word as if it were acid on his tongue, "into the back room and let him think it over."

Viktor lifts the man up easily, chair and all, as if it didn't weigh a thing. He has to be almost seven feet of solid muscle, and he has a certain aura around him that terrifies me. They disappear and Dimitri looks to Anton.

"I heard something in the alley when I was makin' that call," Anton says in a hushed tone.

I can't make out Dimitri's face as he turns away, but my blood runs cold and I pull up so that my head isn't visible from their position any longer.

"You see anyone?"

"Naw, just shadows is all. Could've been a stray bitch for all I know."

There's silence, and I take a deep breath, but then the conversation changes.

"I'm real sorry, boss. He's the only guy that we got that talked to her. She was always real certain on that, that she only ever dealt with one guy. I guess it was so that it didn't get back to you and the Russians. Even I didn't find out until after she was dead, or I would have told you, I swear."

"If she's in debt, he's going to try to collect. From me."

It doesn't seem he's gotten any closer to Rebecca's killer than I have.

I take a chance, glancing down again, and Dimitri

is looking right at me. I go cold, and quickly stand up, gun still in hand. I'm about to head for the door when I hear something that chills me to the spine.

Three gunshots echo through the warehouse. For a second, I think that it's Dimitri, punishing me for spying. Am I dead?

I check my body for bullet holes, as if I'd be more easily able to feel it with my hands than with my pain receptors, and when I find myself whole, all my calm escapes me and I run for the door. I have no idea who it was who fired those shots, or upon whom, and I don't know if I want to find out.

Curiosity really would kill the cat this time.

Curiosity still might have.

CHAPTER 19

Waiting for Dimitri in his condo is the worst decision I've made in the last five hours, since I hightailed it out of the alley. I haven't been able to sleep, the stress and anxiety churning in my stomach.

I should just run. I have no idea what he's going to do to me now that he knows I was following him again. He warned me that I could be killed, but he didn't mean by him, did he?

But I also didn't know he was a killer before tonight. Not for certain. I thought he'd gotten away from those people, and yet here he is: in even deeper.

It makes me want to throw up, but instead I sit on his couch, anxiously wringing my hands. I don't even know why I came here, other than the fact that I have nowhere to go. My life is linked with his, whether I like it or not. If I run, he has the money and motive to find me.

And if I run, who's to say he wouldn't think I'm even guiltier than I am?

That I haven't run to the cops?

Seconds tick by like hours, and when I finally hear his key in the lock, it's sunrise. My back is so tense, I'm not seeing straight. My brain is an absolute fog, and I feel like ducking down, hiding under the couch, just putting off seeing his face for a little while longer.

What if he really kills me? What if this is it? A short, brutal, unhappy life that ends in agony just like Rebecca. Just like my mom and dad.

Tears blur my eyes, and when he pushes the door in, he looks exhausted and enraged. His face is a bit sweaty, his shirt marred with blood, and I hold my breath. He looks at me, daggers in his eyes as he closes the door, locks and bolts it behind him.

The air is sucked out of the room, and we just watch one another. I'm shivering with terror, and when he reaches beneath his jacket and removes a gun, I close my eyes. I'm sure this is it. This one, horrible moment, and it'll all be over.

And then it's not. There's only silence, but for the shifting of his clothing as he walks.

His hand wraps around my bicep, tugging me from the couch so that I'm pressed tightly between him and the edge of the sofa. I can't move, can't get away, and he's glaring at me like I'm the worst person in the world.

This morning I was convinced I was in love with him, and now I wonder if I know him at all.

"How'd you find me, Sarah?" he growls, and when I look down, his other hand collects my chin, making me look up at him.

"Your phone," I murmur, too ashamed to speak any louder. He warned me, didn't he? Why was I so damned stupid as to follow him? I should have just left it alone, especially after finding out that Rebecca was ripping me off.

"You put a tracker on my phone?"

"I wanted to make sure you were okay."

"Damn it, Sarah," he growls, and I'm shaking, wondering what he's going to do. He takes out his phone, handing it to me. "Take it off of my phone. Now."

I unlock it, finding the app and uninstalling it, handing him back the phone. He sets it aside and looks down on me.

"Do you know what would have happened if Viktor saw you?"

"No..."

"You would be in the water with that fucking *goombah*. And do you know what they'd do to me?"

"No."

His finger and thumb hold onto my chin, tightly.

"Viktor would've taken me back to the *Avtoritet*. Do you know what that is?"

I recognize the word, but I shake my head. I have no idea what it is.

"The authority, *da*? The man in charge. I will be seen as a fool for trusting you, and they'll doubt my loyalty to the *bratva*. They would torture me to see if I was actively trying to undermine them. They would use me as a toilet, take a hammer to my fingers, my toes. They would burn me, and when they finally believed me that I had nothing to do with you being there, they would," he pauses, removing his finger from my chin, instead pointing his index and middle finger at his head like a gun. "*Grokhnut*. Just like that, Sarah. You could've gotten yourself, and me, killed tonight. Is that what you wanted?"

I shake my head, my entire body trembling like crazy. I can hardly breathe, and the reality of what has just happened comes crashing down on me. I've had my suspicions, but now I know who — what — Dimitri really is. And what I've just put at risk to find out.

"You're... you're in the mob," I say dumbly, because there's nothing else I know to say. It's all too intense, too terrifying, for me to really comprehend.

His jaw clenches, and I regret asking. When he breathes out, he looks only slightly calmer.

"I am *Bratva*. A *Boevik*. I run my business, they

take what they need. My father was the *Avtorietet* before those Goombah bastards brought the cops down on him. They swore to take care of mother and I with the promise that we'd take care of them down the line."

I feel like I'm going to be nauseous. Why'd I ask? And why's he telling me so much, so freely? That feeling that he's going to kill me once more hangs in my stomach, and I close my eyes just so that I can stop being so dizzy.

His hand tightens around my upper arm, and I can smell the scent of grime and dirt on him.

"What will I do with you now, Sarah?"

"I... I don't know. Please don't kill me," I whimper, the words bubbling past my lips without filter. "I'm so sorry. I never figured... I worried, I was just so worried, especially when I saw you were back with Slava and you asked for my help then pushed me away."

"Because I realized it might've been the fucking Italians, Sarah. I wanted to keep you out of their crosshairs."

"Then why'd you even ask me for help?" I practically scream, tears rolling down my cheeks.

His arms wrap around me, and though it's not gentle, his force, his strong arms, are comforting in their own way. They feel real.

"I thought it was just that dumbass she was dating, or maybe one of her business associates.

When I found out she wasn't just skimming money off me but putting it through the Italians? That's the wrong way, Sarah. We launder their money, not the other way around. She was into something deeper than I imagined and wanted to keep you safe. I should've known better than to think you'd stay where I left you."

I flinch at the disappointment in his voice, and when he pulls away from me, that hardness in his expression is back.

"I'm going to have to teach you a lesson."

There's no humor to his voice, and as much as his words confuse me, they send my heart beating harder in my chest.

"Teach me a lesson?"

"*Da*, Sarah. You apparently didn't take me seriously last time. Apparently telling you that you may be killed isn't enough for you. So you're going to go into my room. You're going to strip. You're going to lay on your stomach, and you're going to wait for me.

My brows knit and I wonder if he's joking. It sounds like some strange, dark, sexual... thing. Teaching me a lesson is one thing, but being naked just adds a level of vulnerability I'm not prepared to cope with.

"Dimitri, I'm really sorry. I get it now. I do. And I'm not going to talk. You know I'm not going to talk."

"If I thought you were going to talk, Sarah, we wouldn't be here right now."

It sends a chill down my spine, and he points to his room.

"I'm not going to tell you twice, Sarah."

His tone is dark and commanding, and I can't refuse it. I'm exhausted, my entire body screaming in agony, but I make my way into his dim, sunlit room and toss my hoodie onto the chair. Next comes my t-shirt and bra, then my dark jeans. My socks and underwear were last, and goosebumps run down my arm with the chill of the air.

Or is it the chill of waiting for what happens next?

I crawl onto his bed as he demanded, but the second my chin hits the mattress, I yawn. I'm so exhausted. Every time I start nodding off, I try to jerk myself up, to be ready for whatever he has in mind.

It's getting to the point where it's impossible to stay awake, though. Where is he? Everything is starting to feel like a terrible dream, like something I'm going to wake up from the next day. Maybe that's all it was. Just a strange, fevered dream.

When I hear his footsteps, I straighten, blinking my groggy eyes open. He's shirtless, changed from his dirty jeans and looking freshly showered. I didn't even hear the water running. Did I doze off?

I gulp, and his dark eyes travel down my body,

tracing over the curves of my shoulders, down into the valley of my back, and over the hills of my ass. He's caressing them with his gaze, memorizing the curves, and I don't know what to make of it but he's making my body burn with desire.

He watches me for so long, and it's driving me crazy. I'm afraid to move, to budge even a muscle and risk displeasing him. How different this is from yesterday, when he held me and kissed me with such tenderness. Now there's just a primal hunger in his gaze, something that I've never seen before.

"Spread your legs."

There's no option for refusal in his tone, and I pull my feet apart, my legs spreading open. I'm so exposed, and it feels so uncomfortable, especially bathed in the early morning light.

He paces to the foot of the bed, and I know he can see me splayed, in a position I've never quite been in before. I have no real idea what he's seeing from his position, but I can imagine.

"Roll back onto your hands and knees."

I do so, and it heightens my awareness of my body. The sensation of a draft passing along my stomach, the way my breasts give way slightly to gravity, my nipples stiffening to the air. But most powerful of all is his invisible gaze, filling me with molten heat.

His voice holds a gravely hardness to it, the lack of sleep affecting him as well.

"Good," he says.

He moves alongside me, his footsteps slow and deliberate as he reaches for the pillows just above my head. Then, one by one, he slides them under my stomach.

I want so bad to ask what he's doing, but I keep my mouth shut. Four pillows in all keep my hips in the air, my legs spread, my pussy on display, and he nods in approval.

"I'm not going to bind you, but if you run, there will be consequences. If you shrink from your punishment, there will be consequences. I can't help that; only you can."

His words are so dark, and yet part of me responds to that primal pull of his. The desire is mounting, but then his knee presses into the bed and his weight joins mine, his pants still casually slung about his hips. His tattoos mark his chest, some of them more faded than others, and he leans his face towards mine.

"Do you understand, Sarah?"

I nod, but I don't know how I can agree to something when I don't even know what it is.

I suppose it comes down to whether I can trust him or not.

His hand touches along my backside and it sends a shiver of excitement down my spine. But when it leaves and comes back with a crack, I let out a squeak in surprise. I'm not sure what I was expecting, but it wasn't his large, heavy hand on my ass!

The sound echoes in my ears, and the air is thick between us, as if the tension is palpable. As if it took on form as soon as that first blow was struck.

Now I'm prone, vulnerable, and my ass smarts. I've been afraid of something worse, of my death, but this is at once erotic and terrifying, because I can feel the barely restrained power in his next strike.

It's calculated, planned, and I buck forward to try to escape it, but I can't.

He grips my shoulders, pulling me back into position. I'm expecting his words, an explanation, something, but his quiet only heightens the uneasy tension in my body. There's no comfort to be found in his dark voice.

I have to take what meaning I can from his hand, from the way he grips me and then smacks the fleshy part of my butt.

I'm robbed of the sight of him, but filled with the knowledge that he can see me. How my ass must be reddening as he bears down for the fourth strike, how my sex is already wet with desire, parted slightly and so vulnerable. The morning light is in full force, bathing me in golden light, and I can't hide anything from him.

Not the whimpers and cries as he spanks me, not the fact that my pussy pulses with need, not how my face contorts just before his blow lands in anticipation of the sharp pain.

Some are lighter, teasing, as if simply keeping me on edge so that I'll never know what to anticipate.

And then there are the hard ones, the ones truly meant for punishment that go through my entire body, pain spreading out like tendrils. He doesn't talk, and neither do I, but for my muddled screams and cries.

The longer he spanks me, the more intense each strike gets. Not just in terms of physical pain, with the varying degrees of power behind them, it always keeps me on my toes and even the lighter ones seem more thrilling.

But it's that the longer he spanks me, the more it fills my other senses. The sound resounds in my mind, the vibrations pass through every bit of my body. I can smell his clean scent, hear his deep, ragged breathing. It's almost like we've become more connected, as if his body is an extension of my own that's been separated, and every blow is us trying in vain to push ourselves back together.

He pauses long enough to grip my hips, to pull me forward so that my ass sticks towards him more. Even a few minutes ago it would have embarrassed me to be so wantonly on display, but now it feels right. Like I'm pleasing him, simply by existing how he wants me to be.

I wiggle my ass a little and he rewards — or

punishes — me with a stronger blow, followed by three lighter ones, and I'm so horny that I can barely breathe. I want him so badly, need to feel that warm, stiff cock up against me.

Is he hard? Is this turning him on, making him strain against his pants with his own desire?

I pray so, and when he spanks me next I moan, pleasure overcoming me, even though when he removes his hand I'm left with a tingling sensation of lingering pain. The idea of taking this punishment and arousing him at the same time is something I've never thought about, but somehow, it turns me on. Is that why I was always spying on him when we were younger?

Was I somehow, subliminally, hoping for this? That he'd hold me and touch me and punish me for being bad?

The thought makes my clit throb and my heart race, and then there's nothing. Dimitri doesn't touch me. I can't even hear him over the sound of my heavy breathing and the blood rushing through my mind. I glance as best I can without moving, but there's not even a shadow left of him.

I swallow, but I don't move. I listen to my heart pounding, feel the tingling, pained sensation on both of my asscheeks and the upper parts of my thighs. I've gone from so much sensation to being deprived of it, and it makes everything else feel and sound more intense.

I strain to hear his movements, but there's no sound.

And then there's a light jingling of metal on metal.

His belt.

The thought sends a chill down my spine, but my legs subconsciously part a bit further, and I lean my ass out, presenting it to him. For his punishment.

My breath is stolen by that first lash of expensive leather against both cheeks. It's sharp and cold, and less controlled than his hand. It doesn't have the personal connection, and I feel both robbed and rewarded. As if this is, truly, the punishment I deserve.

I scream at the second lash of his belt against my ass, my face buried into the comforter as the blows come faster, harder.

They're relentless, blurring together. I barely know what way is up or down. I can't tell if the heavy breathing and screaming is me or just simply noise.

All I know is that my nipples press painfully erect towards the bed, my clit pulsing harder and faster than ever. And when that leather sneaks in between the valley of my thighs, the sharp pain slapping across my pussy, an intense orgasm crashes through me.

I can't hold back, even if I wanted to. It's

completely unexpected and sends me into a shivering, trembling mess as he whips my ass.

When I finally still, he does too, and I hear the belt fall to the floor. The tension has rushed out of me, leaving me floating and light, and I expect his soft touches and warm kisses like yesterday.

I don't get it.

Instead, his two, powerful hands squeeze my asscheeks, pulling them apart. I can feel his breath on my most private of regions, and a tremor of lust runs through me. I'm embarrassed, and excited, all at once.

I try to breathe, to concentrate on not trembling like a leaf, but it's no good and his grip tightens. Already there's so much tenderness in my backside that it's excruciating having that extra pressure, but I can't squirm away. It'll only be worse if I try.

But when he bites my left ass cheek, I don't know whether to laugh or scream, and the noise that escapes my throat is almost a mix of both.

"Dimitri," I whimper, the first words that have been spoken since he ordered me in here. My voice sounds so strange to me, so much huskier and filled with lust. The grogginess from not sleeping probably adds to it.

But I don't get a response. He's intent on torturing me, trapping me in my own mind as my body gives into raw sensation. Refusing me the comfort of his words and dark promises.

Yet there's no way I can anticipate the sensation of his tongue, trailing from the front of my pussy to the back, a growl vibrating my overly sensitive skin.

It's such a sweet caress after such hardness, after the feeling of his harsh hands and wicked belt. For a second I think I'm going to come again, but he pulls away and the sensation fades.

When his thick, throbbing cock suddenly spears me, though, it's a combination of both pain and pleasure. He doesn't ease me into it, let my body adjust to that rigid shaft or how deep he impales me. I've never had sex with him while propped up on pillows like this and it lets him go so much deeper.

Especially with how he pulls my ass cheeks apart, thrusting so hard as to send the ripples through my body.

I'm screaming his name, his brutal thrusts absolutely unforgiving, and every time his hands and hips pound into my ass, a jolt goes through me. When his thumb snakes towards that cleft, though, and I feel it touch along my back entrance, the world suddenly becomes very small.

All I can focus on is that pressure, that building sensation of wrongness. I'm battered and sore, and as that thumb threatens me, my entire body coils like a snake ready to attack.

And then he pops the seal on my body and my vision clouds over. He feels so much bigger in my pussy, that little extra pressure adding to the intensity. It's like I'm on drugs, my entire body shaking and spreading and wanting more and less all at once.

It's intoxicating and it feels so wrong, but I can't squirm away. I'm pinned between him and the pillows that prop me into place, and his other hand goes to my head, gathering hair between his fingers before he tugs.

My body contorts, my spine arches, my breasts brushed by fresh air.

His breathing increases, going ragged and hard, and he growls a word in Russian that I can't make out. He slams into me hard, holding me in place, his body claiming and possessing mine in ways I never could have anticipated.

Fireworks explode behind my eyelids, my pussy tightening around his swollen cock as a second orgasm rips through me. I thought the first was intense, but this one was something on a whole other level. My body is already so sensitive, and as he begins to pump that thumb into my asshole to match the rhythm of his thrusting cock, there's no holding back.

My pussy muscles clench, and he growls, his dick pulsing more rapidly and I know he must be close. His thrusts become faster, more erratic, and then he fucks me to the very depths of oblivion, his cock thrust to my deepest crevice.

His growls of pleasure mix with my screams of ecstasy, and when the spinning world comes back into focus I find his hand has unwound from my hair.

I'm vaguely aware that he didn't come. That he pulled out and there's no hint of his juices running down my inner thigh, and I have to wonder why. I don't know how long we've been in here like this, but my body has a layer of perspiration upon it, and a bead of sweat runs between my shoulder blades.

"Dimitri?" I whimper, trying to look over my shoulder at him and seeing him kneeling over me. He looks like a God, his beautiful features illuminated in the golden sun. It shines along his pecs and biceps, perspiration gleaming and making his tattoos and muscles all the more prominent and glorious.

But when I catch sight of his face and the storm that still rages behind his eyes, I tremble.

He stands, his dick still hard as he walks to his nightstand, opening it up and pulling out a white bottle. He disappears behind me once more. I try not to slump, but I'm exhausted. Every part of my body is awoken to pain, sleeplessness and orgasm both combining to make me drowsy.

My eyelids flutter shut, and I take in a deep breath, coming down from my high.

I hear a lid opening and shutting behind me, but I pay it no mind. I have no control here.

But when his hand spreads my asscheeks once more and cool, viscous fluid touches along my dark pucker, I gasp. It shocks me from tempting, beautiful sleep, but when I try to move, he presses down between my shoulders, holding me in place.

He rubs two digits along my most private of areas, and though they withdraw, seconds later they're back with more of the lube.

"Dimitri," I gasp, uncertain of what to make of the new sensations that threatens to undo me. But when one finger presses into my ass, it sends a strange jolt right to my clit. I'd barely been aware of how the feelings were tied together when he was fucking me, assuming they'd been separate and yet good.

But now my pussy is robbed of any sensation but tingling aftereffects, and still I feel it. That throbbing, that dark, shameful desire. I press in against him, his finger spreading me open, and my lashes flutter down.

I can't handle seeing anything right now. Knowing what I must look like to him as he exposes my every little secret. It's too overwhelming, and he adds another finger slowly, easing me open. I've never felt anything like this, the strangeness of the sensation combatting with the pleasure.

"You've never toyed with yourself," he states, the first thing he's said to me in what feels like eternity. I shake my head, platinum hair mussed up from the blanket and his fist.

"Good. How's that feel?"

"Strange," I say, my voice croaking from hoarseness.

He thrusts his fingers slowly, and I feel his cock bob against my leg, still stiff as a log. It's humiliating and yet at the same time... to know that what he sees turns him on makes it so much nicer. Some of the tension fades from my shoulders as he massages me with his fingers, slowly spreading me open.

It's intense, so intense, and I suck in a breath, holding onto it.

"What do you think I'm going to do?"

"I... I don't know."

"You nearly got yourself killed tonight, Sarah. But I warned you about that already and you didn't listen. Even with your spanking, I doubt that would stop you from doing it again, though it might stop you from sitting for a while. And honestly, I doubt what I'm going to do would stop you either. But ever since you came back into my life, I wanted to make you mine. Wholly. Fully. Every last inch of you."

I shudder, because I want that too. But the darkness in his voice, that hardness, mixed with what I saw him doing earlier...

"Every last hole," he adds with a growl.

If I wasn't so exhausted and turned on and scared, would I run from him? Would I take off, disappear into New York, far from Dimitri and his crimes?

He may have killed someone just hours ago, and

yet here I am, craving for him to defile me in every way imaginable.

His fingers withdraw, and in their place is the throbbing hardness. He rubs along me, slippery and heated. I can't tell if he's simply playing with me or making my nerves come alive, but either way, I love it. I want more.

I've always been a pretty good girl. I made it to my twenties as a virgin, and the worst things I've done have all involved Dimitri.

His hand goes to my back, tracing over the wings between my shoulder blades, the tattoo I wasn't supposed to get. He pauses there, his cock at my rear entrance, and speaks in a graveled tone.

"Beg me, Sarah. Tell me you want this."

I'm torn. Part of me wants it, and not just because I think I deserve punishment. I know I do.

But his words speak to a more primal place, making me ask for something I couldn't ever imagine wanting and yet with him, I do. For him, I do. Because he wants it, and because it turns him on, and because it turns me on too.

I've never been ashamed of my desires, not really, but they've been safely tucked away, forgotten about in the chaos of life until he woke me up again.

"I... I want it, Dimitri," I say softly, my voice quivering with uncertainty that I don't feel. It's just that the words feel strange, that wanting it feels wrong.

His hand cracks against the side of my ass, and

my eyes fly open as I gasp. It's so sharp, and so wrongly delicious.

The same hands that were responsible for brutally beating a man just hours before, maybe even killing him, were used to make my ass sting, to stretch a hole on my body I'd never even imagined giving up to a man. It was a sick, perverse kind of feeling, and he makes me whimper and writhe.

I can feel him pressing that thick crown of his cock against me, my poor little anal pucker stretched by his digits. My spine arches in a feline sort of manner, and my knuckles are white from grasping the bed's blankets so tight, but he's forcing that dark, purple tip into me, and suddenly that warm up — that slow, meticulous easing of my tight little star — seemed like hardly enough.

"C'mon," he growls, using careful force to wedge his girth into that dark crevice of my body, betwixt my two spread ass cheeks.

A searing sensation floods me, the pain and pleasure so intertwined that I can't separate them, even if I wanted to. It was a perfect blend of punishment and reward, and I push back towards him just a half of an inch, enough to make my toes curl and my breathing hitch.

"Oh God," I mutter, my mind a blur. But when his hand dips between the fronts of my thighs, pressing down on my clit, I want him more than anything I've ever wanted in my life.

"Now," I gasp. "Oh God, right now."

But it's not like him pushing into my pussy, it's slower. Much tougher to bear. And even though he's easing that dick into my tight little rear so gently, it's like having a molten rod of steel inserted into my ass. It's excruciating and blissful all at once!

I've never felt so full as when this pulsating shaft of his begins to edge its way into me. He's grunting, grinding his teeth as he pushes in, all that power and strength coiled up in his hardened muscles, being put to careful use as he inserts himself in with the aid of my own pussy's juices and the additional lube. Though I'm hardly aware of that at all, not with him feeding more and more of that thick, veiny girth into me with each passing moment.

Every pulse of his heart makes his cock swell, forcing me open, filling me with sensations I couldn't have imagined.

"Wait!" I gasp when it becomes too much, and he stills, his hand rubbing my clit, distracting me from the pain as well as adding an additional thrum of energy within me. He's careful, even when he's mad at me. Even when he should, by all rights, be rid of the nosy girl that's following him around.

I put him in danger, and yet even now, even taking me in such a primal way, his touch is filled with affection.

"Okay," I breathe out, ready for more.

I instantly regret it though; how could I say I was

ready? There's no such thing as *ready* for his thick, pulsating cock being shoved up my ass! I'm crying out, writhing as he's impaling me upon that large, gorgeous tool of his. And all the while he's giving these low, lewd grunts, his dick bulging with the delighted excitement for claiming me once more.

"*Bozhe Moi*," he curses in a low, guttural voice, so growling and rough. "Tighter than your little pussy even." His fingers toy with my slit, wet little noises emanating as he teases and excites my nerves, trying to distract me from the rod that's sinking in, filling my whole anal cavity.

I topple forwards, grateful for the pillows that keep me propped up. My arms and legs are exhausted, but he's keeping me on the brink of pleasure. Every part of me feels something. The tension between my shoulders, the wet throbbing between my thighs, the rush of my blood in my veins. It all feels so much more significant and I cry out as he settles within me.

It hurts, but it's a good hurt. The kind of hurt I can take for him.

Though each moment I get close to being comfortable with his immense dick lodged within me, a throb of desire passes through his length and I gasp, squirm or shudder. It's a precarious balance, and it can't last long.

In fact, it won't. Because as he grasps my hips tighter, and begins to tug on back, it's that intense feeling all over again. My tacky insides against his slick, lubed up cock; the first insertion done, but it's barely even begun.

He retracts his hand from my clit, and a rough slap cracks across my ass cheek.

"Mmm, I love watching this ass of yours ripple and shake like that," he growls at me, the stinging in my red ass cheeks at least distracting from the intensity of his dick straining my ass.

And his words, his spoken desire... It's like the mess I got myself into last night is finally melting away, and we're back to normal with one another. Back to where we should be. That's worth more than the pain, more than the punishment.

"You're too big," I gasp, my head dizzy with the intoxication of our sex.

He smacks my ass again to remind me of who is in charge; of what matters here. I narrowly avoided death, and compared to that, I suppose having Dimitri's thick, throbbing cock up my ass isn't *so* bad.

Though maybe I should rethink that, because he's thrusting back in now, faster than before and my eyes are rolling back into my head with the intensity of it. A low, guttural sound escaping my throat as he's holding my hips and ass, and making me his.

"Take it," he hisses, sliding his hand back around to pet my aching pussy, to soothe my straining ass. "Be a good little girl for once," he growls as his hips begin to see-saw back and forth, pumping my rear full of his meaty shaft.

The dam breaks, and all the pain and exhaustion is swept away by wave after wave of intense pleasure. I scream into the blanket, my entire body igniting with sensation. I writhe, try to escape him, the ecstasy growing too much, too fast, but it's useless. He's too strong, holding me right where he needs me as my body pulses and clenches his cock.

That tight milking of his shaft makes him moan, and I know he's close. I had him close when he was inside my pussy still. But even as his dick tenses, throbs, he pushes on, building up his pace just a little more, those heavy, cum-laden balls of his smacking against my pussy and clit as he starts to abandon caution. Starts to fuck my ass rougher.

My scream intensifies, as does all the sensations in my body. I almost feel ready to cry, not because it hurts, but just because it is the most intense thing I've ever experienced. Spying on the mob, getting caught, being spanked and fucked by a man that I love?

It's enough to nearly blow my mind.

Or maybe it already has, because as he's pounding my ass, making those cheeks jiggle with each impact, I'm only realizing that I'm already mid-scream, crying out as he's fucking me like a banshee gone wild. All the while he's moaning and tightening that steely grip upon my body, making me his. Completely his.

He pants, gasps, and his leanly muscled body is coated in a sheen of perspiration as he grows closer to his own finale. To the point of no return. Unable to hold it off any longer I can feel him swell within me, straining the narrow little canal of my ass as he's about to blow.

"Take it." He tweaks my clit one final time, pinching that sensitive bundle. "Take it!" he exclaims a mere moment before his balls finish tightening, and he unloads. Thick, creamy streams of his seed blasting into my ass, filling up my rear as I cry out and lose my mind with the blend of sensations, all extreme.

The minutes blur together, his body weight dropped atop mine, both of us spent and exhausted. The sun is high in the sky, and neither of us have slept a wink.

But still, he has enough control over himself to pull back, disappearing to the bathroom and returning with the washcloth. Even after all that, he still cares. He still pampers me.

Cruel, brutal, ruthless. Dimitri's all those things, but he's tender and caring as he uses that warm cloth to clean up the creamy white seed that drools from my gaping hole. He strokes my hair with one hand, leaning in and kissing my temple, all as he tidies away the mess he'd made of my abused little pucker.

"You did very well," he says in a low husky. "When you were not disobeying, that is."

It makes me laugh, and I'm so grateful that the tension between us has faded, at least for now. He leaves for another moment, coming back with a small little ointment bottle, opening it and putting some of the clear jelly on his finger before rubbing it on the fleshy part of my ass where he'd struck.

His powerful hand makes careful little swirls to rub the soothing balm into my flesh, dulling the sting and ache of his punishment. Chasing away the rough edge of its hurt to leave only the twinge of its memory.

Moments later and he's pulling the pillows from beneath me, throwing them back to the head of the bed before he closes the blinds, blocking out the burning sun.

"For now, we sleep. We'll talk about what we're going to do next tonight," he says as he returns to bed with me, tugging my half-conscious body into his. He's so strong and warm, and in seconds, I'm asleep.

CHAPTER 20

When I finally wake up, it's already getting dark, and Dimitri's not in bed with me but I can smell something amazing. I grab one of Dimitri's shirts, my butt still smarting from my earlier punishment. I glance at it in the mirror and see angry red streaks across it, but instead of feeling embarrassed or upset, they bring me a sense of strange calm that I've never felt before.

I pad out to the kitchen where there's takeout bags littered along the table and a banquet atop the fine wood.

"Ah, I figured you'd be waking soon," he says, and his smile is... sweet. That dangerous edge, that anger that I know he felt, has disappeared, replaced with the Dimitri I knew. The sweet, seductive, rebellious Dimitri.

I'm not scared, and that fact is the only thing that bothers me.

"I ordered from Chinar." I recognize it as a Russian restaurant we went to once or twice with our parents.

"I didn't know they delivered."

He shrugs.

"I sent someone."

I raise my brow but don't push it. Instead, I look at the feast before me.

"Dimitri, I can't eat all this."

He shakes his head as he joins me at the table. It hurts to sit, but it's just a reminder of what we've done, what he's done to me, and it sends a thrill to my loins. My nipples stiffen against my shirt, and I pray he doesn't notice.

"You need to eat. To heal up." He begins to point out the dishes to me, making sure I know the difference between the Venison and the rack of lamb, the salmon spring rolls and the smoked duck breast with berries. In the center lay a small tray of what looks like French pastries, and my mouth is watering like mad. I've not eaten in almost a day, and I'm starving.

He pours up two glasses of wine, waiting for me to take my first few bites and moan my appreciation before his expression darkens.

"How long did you stay at the charity ball?"

I can't say I didn't anticipate the interrogation.

"An hour, maybe longer. I ran into Samantha, you remember her?"

He nods, and my gaze falls towards the food.

"Dimitri, did you know my father left me a trust?"

"I had assumed he'd have left you something, *da*."

"She said dad was worth 1.1 billion dollars."

He nods again, as if this were common knowledge. And I guess it is, I'd just never wanted to know. After I lost everything, I tried to cut that part of my life completely out so that I wouldn't miss the money or the ease of living. I told myself it made me stronger to be poor and embrace it, and that lamenting it would just be me living in the past.

"I'm supposed to get it when I turn 21, I guess. And with Rebecca's passing, I guess you're going to get something as well."

He leans back in the chair, looking at me with a calm expression on his face.

"Then we will go see the lawyer in the morning. We've been putting her off for long enough."

My shoulders relax and I take in a deep breath.

"Thanks, Dimitri."

"Sure. We will go in the afternoon, after making an appearance at the office."

The office. I haven't even thought about going back to work. Not that I even really have a job anymore, that I know of. After Rebecca died, after all, my reason for working there disappeared.

The fact that I haven't even wondered about where my rent would come from this month, though, tells me that maybe I didn't distance myself from being wealthy as much as I thought. I'd just assumed Dimitri would take care of me.

My eyes lift to his, and there's so many questions between us, but instead, we continue to eat in silence.

CHAPTER 21

"I'm sorry, Ms. Fairfax, but all that remains in your trust today is five hundred and seventeen thousand dollars. It seems that, without oversight, the trustee withdrew the rest and it is... unaccounted for in her will."

The lawyer's words become fuzzy and I lean back in my chair. Dimitri's hand rests atop of mine in a supportive manner, but I can feel the tension bristling through him.

"That said, she did have numerous business holdings, as well as her investment account which houses six-hundred-million dollars, all of which is left to her sole remaining child, Mr. Brokov."

Dimitri's jaw tenses, and if he could, I'm sure he'd breathe fire.

"I am not her sole remaining child," he sneers, and the mousy lawyer gives me an apologetic smile.

"I'm only reciting what's in her last will and testament. Along with her business holdings and investments, you are also to inherit her Long Island home, and her Cyprus vacation home."

"When will the arrangements be made?"

"Well, Ms. Fairfax will receive the balance of her trust upon her twenty-first birthday, as previously agreed. Unfortunately, if you want the full balance of your original trust, you would traditionally have to have to contest the will, stating that she wasn't allowed to bequeath the money to Mr. Brokov as it was part of your trust."

Dimitri tightens his hand on mine. "It's fine. We can work it out without that," he says, looking at me for my agreement, but it's all too much of a haze. I don't understand.

"Unfortunately, I also have on file a legal contract, signed by you, stating that you will not sue for more money upon being paid the five hundred and seventeen thousand in your trust, and that contract extends to her estate."

The document Rebecca had me sign. I had no idea...

"How much was originally in my trust when my father passed?"

"Eight hundred million. He intended for you to get nearly everything aside from his properties."

I sit back, taking in a deep breath.

"Eight hundred million. She's leaving Dimitri six

hundred million, and there's half a million left in my trust. Where did the rest of the money go?"

The lawyer gives an apologetic, though tight, smile.

"Business investments aren't guaranteed Ms. Fairfax. I'm sure when Mr. Brokov is sent the documents, he will find most of the money is tied up in her businesses and properties. Now, if you'll just sign these documents, I can start the process."

Dimitri looks at me, standing up. Anger darkens his eyes, his entire body seeming coiled like a snake, waiting for his chance to strike.

"Send the documents to my office. I'll review them with my lawyer before signing."

CHAPTER 22

"*D*id you know about this?" I ask, my anger bubbling to the surface despite seeing how pissed off Dimitri is.

He looks offended as he drives us towards his condo, his body still tense.

"Of course I didn't know. I figured your trust was safe and sound."

I sneer out the window, my hand pounding down on the armrest.

"Damn it! It's not even the money, it's that she lied to me! And then she fucking hires me to go work in your company with a promise of a big payoff when that payoff is just my trust. A *fraction* of my trust."

He sighs, his grip still tight on the wheel.

"She must've been embezzling it through her companies and that damned *goombah*. Though embezzling through my own company... She must've been desperate."

"Wait, what?" Rebecca embezzling through Dimitri's company? She'd hired me to look into his books, but I figured he was skimming off the top. That he was laundering dirty money through his company.

He looks at me with a furrowed brow, seeming just as confused as me.

"Sarah... that's why she hired you, isn't it? To get a look at my books, to find loopholes?"

"She never told me why, but I just... I figured you were taking some off the top."

"*Bozhe moi*," he curses under his breath. "Of course I was taking some off the top. That's what I was hired to do. The company is set up to be a legal front. But I was starting to get suspicious after she put me in charge, looking into things too closely. It wasn't adding up, what we were giving to the bosses and what we were bringing in."

"Then why would Rebecca want me looking into it?"

"Because she was skimming off their percent, *Da*? Sending it to those damned Italians. But that money wasn't in her will. It's missing."

I lean back in the passenger seat, watching as the streets of Brooklyn whip by.

"You were hired to spy on me, Sarah?"

"Oh come on, don't be so surprised I'd do that,

Dimitri. Especially after how you abandoned me when Rebecca kicked me out."

A brief hint of sorrow crosses his face, and he pulls over into an alleyway, turning off the vehicle and facing me.

"Sarah, you know why I did that now, right?"

I shake my head. I have ideas, but none that make me feel better about it.

He licks his lips, choosing his words carefully.

"When I got home that night, a few hours after you, mom was up and in the kitchen. She called me in. She asked where I'd been and I lied. I told her I was with my friends, but she saw right through me. I still don't know how, whether she was having me tailed or not, but she knew I was with you. She knew that when I lied, it was because I had something to hide."

I cringe with embarrassment. I had no idea about any of this. Rebecca kicked me out the next morning, and that was the last I ever heard from Dimitri.

"Oh."

"That... that's not all. We got into a fight. I told her that I was leaving the life, the *Bratva*. She'd have none of it. She brought up my father, all the sacrifices he'd made for the family. All the sacrifices she'd made to ensure we would bring more value to the *Bratva*, so that they'd promote me young."

I can't meet his eyes anymore. I know where the story is going. All the pieces are falling into place, and I don't want to hear the rest, but I can't bring myself to interrupt him. His hand goes to my leg, squeezing it in a comforting manner.

"She told me that if I ever contacted you again that she would have you killed. That you're too soft, like your mother, and couldn't handle this life. I guess that's why she wanted to offer you a lump sum payout before your trust matured, so that she could get your signature that said you'd never sue or try to get any more money from her. She wanted you out of our lives forever, Sarah. And I thought... I tried to believe it'd be so easy."

Tears are threatening to spill from my eyes and I try to hold them back. I hate being so emotional, but I can't help it. Not when he's telling me all the reasons why he left me that had nothing to do with me not being good enough. It's such an intense rush of pain and joy, and my breath catches.

"Sarah, I've not been with anyone else since. Sure I flirt, or go to dinner parties, but I never connected with anyone. Not like with you. And when you came back, I hoped it meant that you had Rebecca's blessing. I found out she'd met with you before I saw you in the coffee shop, so I hoped it was safe, even though I knew that with me, you'd never be safe. It's not just Rebecca that'd love to hurt me."

I sob and he squeezes my leg harder, moving in towards me. It's awkward in the car, but he manages to pull me closer.

"Sarah, I've loved you since you were seventeen and you got that tattoo. I've loved you every day since, and it killed me to have to cut you out. But you're still not safe with me."

"I should have a choice about that," I manage out in a soft, uncertain voice. "You can't make it for me."

"I know. I've... I've tried, Sarah, to push you away, but at every turn you're one step ahead. You're smarter than me, and stupider all at once."

It makes me laugh, and his thumb brushes along my cheek.

"I need you, but if you're really smart, you'll walk away. I don't need all that money, and it's rightfully yours. You can take it and start a new life for yourself, find someone safe. Boring, even," he says and I wonder if that's his attempt to dissuade me from listening to him. Some subconscious effort to make me turn away from tedium and run into his dangerous arms.

"Dimitri, I couldn't even stay at the party for an evening. That life isn't for me."

"So? Go, do your own thing. Travel, see the world. Hide your wealth and just do whatever you please. Work as an accountant for the C.I.A. if you want a real rush. Somewhere where you won't get hurt."

I shake my head, and all the tears I've tried to contain start to fall.

"Dimitri, I've missed you so bad. I can't leave

you now."

His thumb wipes away a tear as it rolls down my cheek.

"I've gotten you in too deep because I've been selfish. I've wanted you close. But last night... If Viktor had spotted you, there'd be no way to talk him out of it."

"Then I'll stop. I won't follow you."

"You've promised me that before."

"But now I know, right? I know everything, and... I know there's things I'm better off not knowing."

"You are."

"Please don't make me leave, Dimitri."

He sighs, his large chest rising and falling.

"I can't make you leave this time, Sarah. I can't bring myself to want that. But I want you to leave me for your own good."

"My own good is being with the man I love."

He stares at me, his chocolatey eyes brimming with emotion that I can't read, but when his mouth presses against mine hungrily, all of my barriers crumble down. All of my fears, my apprehension, wash away, and his arms wrap around me urgently.

Though it seems like only seconds have passed before there's a tap at the window, and a stern police officer is looking at us like we've just robbed a bank.

Dimitri and I both laugh nervously as he turns the ignition and slowly backs out onto the road, heading us back towards his place.

CHAPTER 23

I can't believe how lucky I am. I wake up in Dimitri's plush bed, a light breeze pulling me from a happy dream. We'd spent the entire night in one another's arms, and even though he's absent now, there's a note on his pillow.

I smile as I open it up, finding his handwriting.

Sarah,

I've made breakfast for you. It's in the oven to keep warm. I had to head to the office early and you looked like an angel, so I didn't want to wake you. I'm handling the will, and getting you your trust back.

Tonight, I've made a reservation for dinner. Take the day off work if you like and go find something amazing. I'll be home at six to pick you up.

Love,

Dimitri

He makes me feel like a giddy school girl, and

beneath the note is his black AmEx card. I swing my legs, pulling myself reluctantly out of bed. It's so comfortable, but at the same time, I'm looking forward to doing a bit of shopping.

Last time it was for the event I didn't want to go to. This time it's to knock his socks off for a dinner date.

The smell of breakfast is rich in the air, and I head to the fridge to grab a glass of orange juice. Opening the oven, I find eggs, bacon and pancakes, all arranged into a cheesy smiley face. I giggle as I take it out, putting it on the table and taking a moment to really say thanks for how perfect life is.

No sooner had I lifted my fork, though, that my world goes black.

CHAPTER 24

*W*hoever it was has been quiet, and prepared, because I never heard the slightest sound as they got behind me. Never felt or suspected a thing until that black sheet is wrapped about my face and pulled back. I am gagged and blinded at once, and their strong grip doesn't allow for me to get away.

I kick out my legs and grab at the material, but now I'm restrained. There must be more than one of them, but I'm panicking, flailing, and they're strong. Practiced.

In my panic I strike the table with my foot, and I hear the jarring sound of the plates and utensils shifting. My would-be captors are tying my hands and yanking me back, but I strike out again randomly, and kick the table hard, sending dishes crashing to the floor, smashing.

My muffled cries don't do much but make me panic more, I can't even call out, everything feels so futile!

I'm being dragged across the floor, over the carpet and towards the door, but before we get there I can feel one of them pinning down my legs beneath his weight, and wrapping something about them. It's painfully tight, restricting me, pinching my flesh.

"Stuff her in the bag," I hear, the words gruff and perfunctory. As if abducting me is just some tedious task in their routine.

I'm panicking even worse at that as their arms retract, but even still, bound as I am about the face, arms and legs, all I can do is rock from side to side. I can't see a thing, but I hear a long zipper open, and then I'm picked up from the shoulders and feet, lifted and then placed down inside some large, thick bag with a stiff bottom.

Then, just like that, they shove something else into my mouth, through the black cloth, tie it at the back of my head, silencing even my pathetically muffled cries, and the zipper tears shut.

And that's that.

I'm hoisted up and trotted out, like some piece of furniture on moving day.

The bumping and jostling as I'm taken out into the hallway, to the elevator and then out onto the streets is only minor. It's when they throw me into the back of some vehicle and my head bangs off the bottom of the bag painfully. *Where is the doorman? How's this happening to me?*

Doors slam shut and like that, I'm off. To god knows where.

And Dimitri won't even know I'm gone for hours.

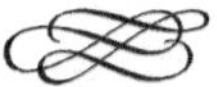

CHAPTER 25

It smells... sterile. Like that weird scent of a doctor's office; bleach and other cleaning solutions muddled together into a different sort of funk. It's unpleasant, yet I'm trying to gasp for breath, the bag and the hood all stifling my ability to breathe.

Not to mention the panic.

Tears soak the bag, but no matter how much I struggle, I'm trapped.

I can hear at least two men speaking in Russian, and my blood runs cold. Is this what Dimitri was warning me about? Did Viktor see me, and this is the end? Everything was so perfect, my life was just getting on track, and now it's over.

I sob, and there's a firm kick to my ribs. It steals my breath, and my eyes widen, looking at the dark nothingness before me. I'm all alone, no one knows where to find me, and I can almost smell the death in the air.

Is this where the Italian accountant was killed? It's cold, and that would explain the smell of bleach. I can't even beg for my life, though, with this gag in my mouth.

I hear more talking in Russian, and then the bag is unzipped, and very abruptly I am yanked out of it and lifted up. But not all the way, the two men holding my arms let my legs drag upon cold cement floors before I'm shoved down into a hard, metal chair. It's a rough move, they slam me down so recklessly and without missing a beat I can feel handcuffs strapped to the chair and then me, both at my wrist and ankle.

More muttering in Russian, and then the gag is stripped away, and with a sudden yank the black cloth is taken off and I'm blinded by a bright light shining directly into my eyes.

"You think someone with your ties would know better than to stick your pretty little nose into a man's serious business," comes the harshly accented voice. But as I'm blinking my eyes and struggling to see, he slaps me across the face, hard, and I'm reeling and sputtering.

My body stings and burns as I struggle to get a better grasp of where I am. There's no windows, no light except for the one burning my retinas.

"I don't know anything, I swear," and I find it so

much easier to lie with conviction when it's poten-tially life or death. I'll say anything to get out of here. Anything!

"That no longer matters," he says so casually, grasping a hold of my hair, coiling it about his fingers as he cruelly twists and forces me to stare up at him and the light. "You stuck your nose into the boss's business, and now it's too late for questions about what you know. You're a risk," he says, almost hissing the final words.

Oh God. This is it. I close my eyes to hide my fear, so that I can pretend I'm anywhere but here. I think of how my day was going to be, buying a dress to make Dimitri's jaw drop before he takes me out on the town. I imagine him coming home to find his apartment ransacked and me missing. He'll know exactly what happened, and will blame himself.

"Please, please. I have money. Lots. I'll give it to you," I plead desperately.

"Little rich girl," he says with such scorn, "money will not solve all your problems."

And then, through my bleary eyes, I see Dimitri. Like an angel arisen to come save me, he pierces even that murky, hard-to-see film of tears.

"We caught this one trying to sneak in," says the guard with a gun to Dimitri's back, shoving him along.

I hear more Russian cursing, then the guy in front of me speaks loudly:

"How did he find us? Huh? You idiots," he curses again.

"He was following us all the while, must have arrived just as we were making off with her," explained the other man. But my eyes were solely for Dimitri then.

I blink away the tears to see him, standing there, half-business executive hunk, half disheveled would-be rescuer.

And yet now we're both here, caught and soon to be dead.

"Dimitri," I whimper, leaning towards him the fraction of an inch that my bindings allow, as if just being nearer to him would make this all go away. "You shouldn't have come."

"He really shouldn't have," my captor says, a smug look on his face as he cracks his knuckles.

"Don't worry, Sarah," Dimitri says, sounding so calm. "I'll have you out of here in just a moment."

"The fuck you will!" says one of the brutes, and the guy with a gun to Dimitri's back draws back his hand and strikes Dimitri in the face with the butt of the gun.

From there, everything happens so fast I can barely even fathom it.

Dimitri takes the hit, and I hear a crack as his broad jaw reels from the blow. My cry fills the air, but then without missing a beat, Dimitri takes hold of the man's arm holding the gun with both hands.

He head-butts the guy, twice, in quick succession, and a spray of red blood spurts out, covering Dimitri's once expensive and stylish suit.

I stare in shock, as in mere fractions of moments it all unfolds.

The guy to Dimitri's right comes at him, reaching out and grasping the back of his hair and yanking on his head. But Dimitri pries the gun from the other man's hand that he holds tight, and fires off three shots into this guy's torso.

Cursing fills the air, but Dimitri's movements are swift and precise. He turns the gun back on the guy he bashed open the nose of, a single shot rings out as he fires up beneath his jaw, blowing out the top of his head in a gory mess.

But no matter how fast and sure Dimitri is, there's still two guys to one of him. The other thug comes at him, but as Dimitri raises the pistol to fire, he bashes down on Dimitri's arm, so he can't fire at him.

Dimitri's undeterred though, and as if he saw that coming, his free hand rockets up and he punches the guy right in the throat. One brutally hard punch and the man is choking, eyes wide.

I watch in horror as the lead thug in front of me pulls out his own gun, slower than the others, clearly not used to getting his hands dirty quite so often as his henchmen. But before he can get a shot off, Dimitri pulls the other guy down and rams his knee up into the man's face, breaking another nose and sending another spurt of blood across his pants.

Shots ring out, and I know they're not Dimitri's. It's the creep in front of me, but they miss their mark. Dimitri's not sitting still for half a second, constantly in motion.

The head gangster is angry, he's fired off twice, but Dimitri spun around, taking cover behind the brutalized man. He shouts out in a fit of rage:

"Stop or I'll—" he doesn't get to finish his words, or even point the gun at me to complete his threat before Dimitri unloads five rounds into him.

Like that, it is all over.

The most gruesome and gory scene I had ever imagined occurred, and it lasted but a few seconds. A brief, ghastly rescue, where Dimitri went from captive to savior.

A final shot and he ends the dying thug he'd hid behind, and then he comes to me, running a hand back over his sleek, tousled hair. He rummages through the leader's pockets, grabbing the keys to the handcuffs.

His motions are seemingly calm, smooth, calculated, but as he comes to me to untie my binds, I can see that faint cracks in his facade. He killed four men to rescue me, and did so with a precision and practiced grace that stuns me. But he's not unshaken.

"Are you alright?" he asks, and there's some worry in his voice. This time he wasn't fighting for survival, he was fighting for me. And that changes the equation. It changes everything. Made the stakes so much higher than he was used to. I could tell that just by the sound of his voice, the look in his eyes.

There's blood and gore all around me, but I beg myself not to look at it. Instead. I focus on him, on the fear and anguish in his eyes, and I truly understand why he'd tried to push me away all those years ago. He never wanted to feel this, to have me grasped by his life.

I nod, but I need to get out of here. I need to run from the smell of coppery blood and bleach, from the reality of what's just happened. My arms wrap around his neck, and I can barely stand or walk I'm so badly shaken.

It's horrible. I've never seen anything like it, and I want to throw up.

Dimitri picks me up into his arms as if it was nothing, the most casual of things. But as he's carrying me towards the stairs to exit, we hear the sound of the heavy metal door down the stairwell swing open and he rushes to the side, and just in the nick of time.

The door to the room soon after is jarred open, and we only got behind it barely. Dimitri puts me down as we watch a thick, stocky goon push his way past, gun pointed and at the ready.

But he's not looking the right way, and Dimitri

swings his own gun up just in time to fire and put an end to him in a spray of red.

Another guy emerges out of the stairwell behind the first, and he grabs Dimitri's arm, pulling it down and twisting the gun away. He rounds the corner, pointing his own gun at me and for a brief flicker of a moment I think it's all over as I hear a gunshot go off.

But Dimitri grasps the other man's arm in return, pushing him wide, and the bullet is fired just to the left of my shoulder, causing me to cry out.

The two are grappling, but Dimitri's gun is knocked away!

"No!" I shout, but it was a false alarm.

Instead, he just drops it, and rather than trying to shoot the man he twists his arm free and punches the guy in the gut. It's enough to knock the wind from him before he head-butts the man. He crumples lower, his arm pointing up now, but the gun still pointed away from either Dimitri or I.

It becomes a contest of raw strength until Dimitri knees the guy in the face, then raises his leg up. While holding the man's two arms, Dimitri kicks down into his throat, stomping it in until he's down on his back and finally… his limbs go limp.

I've never seen anything so gruesome as I have in the last few minutes, and I clutch the wall as my stomach tries to bring up the bile in my throat. I haven't eaten for so long, though, and there's nothing to throw up no matter how much my body wants to.

Dimitri simply pries the gun from the guy's hand and holds it at the ready as he reaches out, taking hold of my hand.

"Come on. Let's not linger here any longer, Sarah," he says urgently, pulling me around the door and down the stairs as he hurries us along the cold, empty stairwell.

He keeps his gun ready to fire, but as we reach the bottom of the stairs and he cautiously peeks out along each direction of the street outside, he dashes out with me in tow. It's not long before we come to his car, parked just around the corner, and he casts off the gun into an alleyway dumpster before helping me into the car then hopping into the driver seat.

I'm shaking, but I brush off Dimitri's concerns. I don't want to be near this any longer than he does.

So many thoughts are rushing through my mind, and yet I can't focus on any one long enough to actually speak. I rock myself back and forth in the passenger seat as he pulls onto the road. I don't know where he's headed, but I just want to be away from it all.

I look down and notice there's blood spattered on me, and it makes me dry heave again, my hand gripped so tight on the armrest that my knuckles are turning white.

Dimitri glances at me, concern evident in his expression, but he must realize how bad I need to get to a shower. He turns onto a more familiar road, heading back to my place as it's nearer.

We don't talk the rest of the way home. What is there to say? There's no way to bring what I just saw into words, my feelings of fear and anguish and disgusted relief all rushing like a tsunami within my heart.

He saved me, but at such a high cost.

He's a killer.

Some part of me knew it all along. The part that watched as he and Slava kicked the shit out of Anton knew it was a possibility. That it would escalate, become something more terrifying. I didn't want to admit it to myself, but now, there's no denying I knew what he was.

It's not that he killed those men. It's that those weren't the first men he killed. He was too quick, too practiced, for that to be his first time. And now, he seems on edge, but I have a feeling that it's more about his concern for me.

I glance over at him, the harsh, mid-day light making the shadows on his face more dramatic. He's driving cautiously, trying not to alert anyone to our bodies still marred with blood, and when he finally pulls up to my house, we both breathe a sigh of relief.

"Joanna won't be home, she's at work," I say and

he nods, exiting the vehicle and opening my door for me. I don't have the keys, but I go to my bedroom window and wriggle it up. It's never locked right, despite me complaining to the landlord a dozen times, and for once I'm grateful that she's lazy.

Dimitri slips in after me, glancing around my room. It's plain, bare, and to him it must look pathetic. Like a poor college girl's dorm, dank and slightly smelling of mildew.

"I'll wait," he says simply, I guess because he wants to give me time alone to process what just happened. To give me an out, in case I want to run. In case I can't handle who he really is.

He has no way of knowing that I've known all along. That his violence, his connections, at once drew me in and repelled me, a powerful force keeping me in his orbit.

"You can join me," I say gently, and it's the most surreal moment. Both of us covered in blood spatter, standing in my dark bedroom, and that tension between us growing to a fevered pitch.

His hand clasps my face before I can move, his mouth finding mine. Seconds later and both of his hands are beneath my ass, hoisting me up and pressing me against the wall. I'm trapped between him and it, his heart pounding fast against his ribs.

I feel his hardness throb against me, and I grind back, making him growl his approval. Pulling me from the wall, he heads towards the bathroom with my guidance, but we barely separate for more than a second as we turn the water on and strip free of our bloody clothes.

Adrenaline is still pumping through me, and when we get into the shower, the warm water hitting our naked bodies, we're like animals groping at one another. I just want to feel him on me, all over me. To know his body, his strength, and embrace how fucked up I am over him.

My arms wrap around his neck and we kiss, hard and passionate, his erection grinding against my stomach.

"Dimitri," I whimper, and his arms tighten around me as if he instinctively knows what I need. That I want to feel his protection, that I want to know his strength.

"I got you," he murmurs against my ear before biting it hard. "I was afraid I'd never see you again."

I gulp, and he kisses down to the hollow of my neck, water pouring over his hair.

"I was so scared you'd come home tonight and see it was too late. Why were you home so early?"

"I'd just gotten back from the meeting with the lawyer and wanted to let you know how it went. When I saw the security guard knocked out, I worried it'd be you so I waited to see."

"I'm so glad you did. I was so scared you wouldn't find out until tonight..."

He suckled my clean skin in response, his hand

running over my hips and ass, gentle so as not to hurt my bruised flesh.

How can he be so considerate and kind while still being so cold? There's not a hint of regret on his face, or in his actions. He's justified, vindicated, and just having me in his hands is enough.

"I'd never let them hurt you," he murmurs into my flesh before he moves me, settling me onto the floor of the tub. The water pours over us like a warm rainfall, absolving us of our sins as his stiff erection prods my belly.

It's cramped, but neither of us minds as he presses into me, making us one once more.

"Oh God," I gasp, and he takes no time before thrusting into me harder, faster. There's no teasing, no games, only our bodies meeting in a frenzy of need and desire. My legs wrap around him, slippery from the water, and I'm already so turned on that he meets no resistance.

It scares me how horny I am, how much I need this intimacy in the face of danger. Maybe that's all it is. I nearly died, and now I need to feel alive. But deep down, I know it's something more than that. Something I can't bring myself to dwell on.

"I thought I almost lost you," he growls, and I feel him swell within me. "I won't let anyone take you from me, not ever!"

My head rests against the rim of the tub as he presses me forward, his grunts and groans echoing off the walls of the shower. The erotic sounds fill my ears, my senses overcome with arousal.

"Dimitri!" I whimper as his hand goes to my breast, rubbing my nipple until it's stiff before pinching and tugging it.

The pain excites me, and I scream louder, the sound reverberating through me.

And when we're finally left in a writhing, pleasured mess, and cold water is pounding down on us, I finally feel that clarity I've been seeking. That I can accept him, for who he is. For the risks it brings me, for the anxiety and fear.

I belong with him.

Grinning, he helps me up, his skin covered in goosebumps from the chilly water, and he wraps his large arms around me.

The knock at the door startles us out of our pleasant afterglow.

"Sarah, you almost done in there? I gotta pee." Joanna's voice sounds strained, on the brink of a giggle fit, and I blush brilliantly.

"Y-yea! Just a second."

I glance at Dimitri as I step out of the tub, and his dark eyes twinkle with devious delight. I toss him a towel before wrapping myself in one as well, picking up our blood stained clothes.

"Sorry," I mutter as I open the door, my face still burning with embarrassment. "Figured you were at work."

"Yea, but I come home for lunch, remember?" She pushes past me, though not before looking Dimitri up and down, the towel slung around his hips not leaving much to the imagination. He bows his head before he follows after me, back into the privacy of my bedroom.

"Well, that was embarrassing..."

"Why?" Dimitri asks, shutting the door behind us.

"She probably heard everything."

He shrugs his heavy shoulders.

"Not the worst thing we could have been caught doing today."

"Yea... Fuck, you warned me. I can't say you didn't."

"No, you can't."

"I knew I should have just walked away, like, a million times. But after I saw you at the cafe, and realized you were involved with Slava again..."

For some reason, that makes him pause.

"The cafe... That day you followed me, in the rain?"

"Yea. I mean, I saw that Slava was calling you again, and I had a bad feeling. When I saw him go into the cafe after you left, I figured out that the owner must be an intermediary and I just got really worried about what you two are into. I guess for good reason," I say with a sigh, grabbing a simple t-shirt from my dresser. "I don't have a change of clothes for y—."

I can't finish my sentence as his heavy hand bears down on my shoulder and he spins me to look at him.

"Sarah, you're telling me you saw Slava go into that building?"

His tone makes my blood run cold.

"Yes. Just after you left. I figured it was a drop site."

His jaw tenses.

"You took pictures of this?"

"Yea..."

"And you're absolutely positive it was him? It couldn't have been anyone else?"

"No. I mean, I don't think so. I remember him really well, Dimitri. He was always over at the house."

He sucks air through his teeth, his face reddening.

"What's wrong?"

"Slava isn't supposed to have anything to do with that cafe. That is my contact for doing what I do. He's not even supposed to know it exists."

"But... what does that mean?"

"No one is to have contact with the *Kassir* but for the *Avtoritet*, hm? But he was a family friend. My father and mother go way back with him, and he always took care of us. So I take care of him, on top of what I give to the *Avtoritet*. Slava isn't even to know he exists."

"What would Slava want with him?"

"He handles all the money. If Slava was going to him and I didn't hear about it..."

"Dimitri... that was right before we found out Rebecca was killed. Only an hour or two had passed before we got the call."

Dimitri's face hardens into stone, his body rippling with muscles, hidden only by the towel still at his waist.

"It was Slava's guys that had you. I thought maybe Slava was tailing me again, and that's how they knew you were there that night. That capturing you was revenge for you spying. But if he's going behind my back..."

"We need to find him and stop him, Dimitri! If he killed Rebecca and tried to have me killed..."

He nods, grabbing for his phone.

"We need to get back to my place. Now."

CHAPTER 26

His condo looks even worse than I anticipated. Apparently I'd done some real damage when I was captured. Worse still is the now stale smell of breakfast that reminds me how I still haven't eaten.

Dimitri's talking on his phone in Russian, and getting angrier by the second as he starts throwing clothes into a suitcase.

I grab a bag to start packing my own stuff, but he puts a hand on it and shakes his head no before motioning me out of the room. I'm too exhausted and hungry to put up a fight, so I grab something from the fridge, eating quickly to calm my gnawing hunger.

I don't know how long it is before he comes out of the room, but he looks angry as hell, and I can't help but cringe a little from his rage.

"Slava's gone. He knows he fucked up, and he's on the run."

"Well that's good, isn't it? I mean, if he's not here to cause us more trouble..."

"He won't stop. Once he's set his sight on something, that's it, Sarah. I have to go after him."

I knew it was coming but it still stings.

"Dimitri, you can't."

"Yes, Sarah, I can, and I will. I don't have time to argue with you. I have to head to the airport."

"Let me come with you."

His hands ball into fists and he stares at me.

"If you're there, I'm just going to be worried about you the entire time."

"And if I'm here, alone, surrounded by the mob? We don't know who's on his side, Dimitri!"

That makes him stop for a second, so I keep going.

"I know he's not going to stop. I saw you, that night. After dad died, and you and Slava went to punish Anton. You took the truck for some reason, and I was in the back, sleeping. I know what he's capable of. I know what *you're* capable of. But I'm still here."

"*Bozhe moi*," he curses that now familiar saying, and he takes a few steps towards me. For a second, I'm afraid of what he's going to do now that he knows my secret, but instead he simply nods.

"Fine. Go. Pack. I'm not leaving you here unprotected, and I don't know who Slava's polluted with his corruption."

I move quickly to the bedroom and he barks orders behind me.

"Dress light, but bring some black with you. Your camera too, with the biggest lens you have. We're going to have to play this careful. He's being unpredictable. I've never known him to run from a fight before."

I nod, tossing everything I can into a bag.

"So where's he going?"

"Cyprus. He has friends there. Friends that will hide him."

CHAPTER 27

*R*ebecca had a vacation home in Cyprus, though to call it a vacation home is an understatement. The modern villa has a beach lounge, a spa, and a Presidential Suite to die for. I've only been here once before on a family vacation, but now it all seems so different.

When I was a kid, it was just another place, and I complained about the morning sun waking me up. Now I'm taken aback by the luxury and the ostentatious interior.

But this is not a vacation, and the tension in the air infects even the most beautiful and lavish of rooms. Dimitri has been pacing since we arrived, calling his local contacts and trying to find Slava without Slava knowing. It's harder than I anticipated, and way more boring.

I've done a few stakeouts on my own, but it

doesn't feel right, being in such a beautiful place and not being able to enjoy it.

Dimitri comes out of the room, giving me a half-hearted smile before he joins me on the couch.

"This is going to take some time. He's likely deep in hiding now."

I nod. "Sure, Dimitri. So what do we do now?"

"I have some money in the bank here. I'd like to give it to you to tide you over before your trust kicks in. It's untraceable."

"Dimitri, you don't have to..."

"I know. But no one knows of these accounts, and if something happens to me, I don't want the money to disappear into banker's pockets."

My lip quivers, but I nod. It's a distraction, and that's what we need. We landed hours ago and have gotten nothing accomplished. All we know is that Slava landed at Nicosia Airport just ahead of us, and he's likely in Limassol. Apparently that's where most of the Russian Mafia has property.

"Fine, but can we grab dinner out?"

His expression softens and he nods.

"Of course, Sarah. I'd give you everything if I could. Anything that you want. And once Slava is taken care of, then we will be free, and mother will be vindicated."

"You're sure it was Slava that killed her?"

"*Da*. I had a feeling things had gotten strange between them, but had no idea why. The accountant, he had said some things that raised my suspicions, but I had no proof until you told me what you'd seen."

"I'm really sorry. I know you two were close."

"We were. But no one lays a hand on what's mine without paying for it," he says, reaching across and caressing my cheek with the back of his hand. "He will pay with his life for scaring you."

I bite in on my lower lip and Dimitri's head tilts, his gaze trailing over my face before he stands.

"We will talk more about this tonight," he says before helping me up from the couch. "For now, go get changed, and we'll go to dinner as if this the romantic date I owe you."

His mouth presses against mine, briefly, and though there's still so much to say, I go and get changed.

* * *

THE SKY IS a brilliant navy blue, the moon peeking up from the horizon, and the coolness of evening meets the heat of the day. The restaurant Dimitri takes me to is gorgeous, and we're sat outside, fragrant flowers illuminated under sparkling lights.

The last twenty four hours has been terrifying, and there's been a knot of tension in my stomach ever since, but as I let the warm, Cyprus air caress me, I start to feel like a human again.

Dimitri's dressed in a white button-down shirt, and he looks almost as good in clothes as he does naked. Almost. The shirt still strains against his muscles, and his smile twinkles to his eyes.

"I was expecting we'd do this back in the city, but this is even nicer," he says, relaxing back in his chair. "I will have to thank Slava for that one thing."

The fact that he's speaking so casually about a man he's planning on killing disarms me, but I'm not repulsed by it. I should be, but I'm not.

It feels so wrong that it doesn't feel wrong.

I cross my legs and Dimitri leans in, his eyes sparkling. Our dishes are cleared away and we're just waiting on our dessert. Everything is so terrible and perfect all at once.

Sure, if you can ignore Dimitri's involvement in the Russian Mafia, and pretend you're both on vacation rather than planning to kill someone, life's wonderful, my brain sarcastically muses.

But when Dimitri reaches into his pocket, and takes out a small, black, velvet box, my thoughts go silent. It feels like the world has stopped, the conversations at the nearby tables fading into the background. Everything has grown quiet and slow.

When he opens the box and reveals the most beautiful ring I've ever seen, my heart stops.

"I know this is sudden, but the second you walked back into my life, I knew that was it for me. I wanted to do this last night, but I can't think of a more perfect place to ask. Sarah, will you be mine?"

Tears flood my cheeks, all of the tension and stress washed away with the tenderness of his words. The beautiful stone catches the light, little diamonds surrounding the blue sapphire. I reach out, my fingertips grazing over it, and never have I wanted something — someone — so bad.

"Dimitri, of course!" I cry out, nearly knocking the table over as I lunge towards him, my arms wrapping around his neck.

He laughs, picking me up and holding me to his chest as his mouth moves against mine. The restaurant bursts into applause, and I don't even care that they're all watching as we make out. I'm going to get married! To Dimitri!

He lifts me up, spinning me around, and I've never seen him look so damn happy in my life. We're reduced to giggling, giddy messes, and when the waiter returns, it's with a bottle of wine and the most delectable pastries.

Dimitri settles me back on the ground, putting the ring on my finger, and for the rest of the meal, all I can think of is getting him back to the villa and really celebrating.

"I CALLED IN A FAVOR," Dimitri explains to me as a tired looking banker unlocks the building.

It's already after ten, and even with the jetlag, I'm buzzed. Excitement courses through my veins along with the wine, and I can't stand still.

Dimitri laughs, putting his hand on my hip before kissing me.

"Calm down. We'll be home soon," he says with a smile. But when he stands up and looks over my shoulder, his entire demeanor changes. What he sees literally sobers him, and before I know what's happening, he sets off running.

Just like that our moment of peace, our brief little fantasy of being a normal couple, vanishes.

"Dimitri!" I cry out in surprise. When I spin around I see Dimitri in fast pursuit of Slava. The dark, narrow streets don't give either of them much leeway.

"Where's he going?" asks the banker.

"Wait here!" I shout as I take off my high heels and sprint in their direction.

Dimitri reaches for the back of his pants, grasping his gun.

I'm behind them though, and I can barely catch a glimpse of the two sprinting men. Dimitri's almost as fast as he is strong, after all, but Slava is fueled with terror.

Dimitri's gun is out as his legs pump, but he can't get a clear shot. Every time he's lining it up, Slava darts down another turn. It's frustrating for me just to watch, but I know it's too dangerous to risk a shot. We're in another country, and we don't know the place, what if a stray bullet hits someone?

Slava runs out of the alleyway and into the streets, and though the hour was late the night crowd was out. Dimitri has to lower his gun, hide it in his jacket as he pushes past the people. One woman on a bike nearly crashes into Dimitri, but he dodges out of the way in time, while Slava is hit by her riding companion who goes toppling into the road.

It isn't enough to stop Slava though, and he scrambles up and across the street onto the sidewalk.

The chase carries on, and I have to make my way across the street to horns honking angrily at me. Luckily the two men created enough commotion that it's stalled traffic so I can get by safely.

Slava shoves a man down so that Dimitri has to leap over him, and Dimitri is clearly losing his patience as he hauls his gun back out. Slava dashes down into an alleyway again before he can use it.

It takes me a few moments more before I can get there, but once I do I arrive in time to see Slava encounter two people in the alleyway. It's a cop and some criminal he's arresting, but instead of calling for help, Slava grabs the officer, slams his face to the wall, seeming to knock him out as he pulls the gun from the cop's holster.

Dimitri acts fast though and fires. Screams fill the night as people hear the gunshot, and then Slava cries out in pain.

Slava's gun clatters to the ground and he turns to run again. Dimitri fires once more, but Slava's gait is uneven and the shot misses, instead hitting the cement wall.

Dimitri's closing in on him, running past the cowering crook and the battered officer and back out into the streets after Slava. It's no longer safe to shoot but he's nearly got him as Slava's pace slows while cradling his wounded, bleeding arm.

He's just a few paces away, but then as Slava rushes into the streets a bus barrels past, kicking up dirt and dust.

Dimitri comes to an abrupt halt, narrowly avoiding crashing into the vehicle. But it's not the last; two more busses pouring out of the shopping center all at once come by, and Dimitri is fuming. His gun is tucked into his coat, hand still grasping it, but even as I get beside him, neither of us can see any sign of Slava in the brief glimpses between the busses.

When finally they're gone, we're left standing, facing an empty side of the street. I can barely catch my breath, my hand going to Dimitri's arm.

"Wait," I say, "the blood trail!" It's dark, with only

the street lights to guide us, but with some effort I can see the dark blood in the moonlight.

Dimitri's beside me, vigilant as I look at the inky-black droplets of blood on the pavement and then sidewalk. We follow it across the road until…

It just stops.

"Dammit!" Dimitri curses as we trace the blood off the sidewalk, where it just ends in the road, as if he'd climbed aboard a car and disappeared.

I slump, defeated, before looking up at Dimitri.

"He knows we're here now," he says with a sneer. "We need to find out where he's staying."

A lightbulb goes off in my head. Joanna might be just the woman to help.

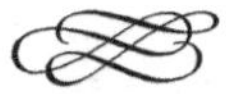

CHAPTER 28

"Hey, Joanna?"

"Sarah? What's up? You didn't come home last night."

Oh, right. This is awkward. How to tell your roommate you ran off to Cyprus on a private jet at the last minute?

"It's a really, really long story and I'll tell you all about it soon, but I need a favor."

"A favor?"

"You know how much you love background check stuff?"

"Uh-huh."

"Well... I need you to do something for me. I need you to find out where someone owns property in Cyprus. Limassol is the town. The problem is that he might have bought it in cash, outright. The owner is Slava Romonov."

I hear her typing, along with all the unasked questions lingering between us.

"Jeez, first hit is that he did time for being an enforcer in the Russian Mafia?"

"Yea... Yea, that's him. How long do you think it'll take?"

"Well, if he paid cash, I'm probably going to have to do a lot more digging, but you know me. I love a challenge!" she says, chipper as ever. "When are you coming home?"

"Probably not for a little while. Just give me a call when you find something out?"

"Aye-aye, roommate. Are you with Dimitri?"

"Yea."

She lets out a low whistle.

"I still can't get the image of him in that towel out of my head."

I glance over at Dimitri who's pacing behind me, his brow furrowed in thought. My thumb runs over my engagement ring and smile. I'll tell her about all this later.

"Me neither," I admit. "I'd really appreciate if you could come back with something fast. It's important."

* * *

DIMITRI LOOMS over me on the bed, his dark eyes still sparkling with lust as our bodies grind together in the aftermath of our lovemaking. It's early morning, but both of us are jet lagged and running on adrenaline.

"Every time I look at you, you seem too good for this world," he murmurs with a bit of gravel to his voice. His fingers gently stroke along my cheek bone, around the shell of my ear as he tucks my blonde hair behind it.

"Dimitri..." It makes my heart pitter when he talks like this, and I quiet him with a gentle kiss.

"I'm serious," he breathes against my lips. "You're too good for me. I'll never know why you came back to get wrapped up in all this shit."

"Well... I didn't really know that I'd be surrounded by murder and death."

"True," he says as his thumb traces along my lower lip. "But you know now. And you're still here. If it'd been any other girl, she'd have thrown up and run the other way. Run to the cops. Something."

"It's never even occurred to me..."

"I know it hasn't. But maybe it should have. Maybe it still will."

I shake my head, his weight pressing down on me.

"Dimitri, you just proposed, and I just said yes. I'm not going anywhere. I love you."

"How can you love someone like me?"

"It's easy. I know you'll never hurt me. That you'll never do anything to hurt me. Isn't that what everyone wants? Someone to protect them and make them feel wanted? Desired? You do all of that and more. It's not... pretty, but Dimitri, it's not like you killed those guys for no reason. They were bad guys."

"To them, I'm the bad guy."

"Well," I say, my hand going to his bare back, tracing over the angel wings he has there that match mine. "They're wrong."

He kisses me, hunger and passion driving him as his body envelopes mine.

"Once I take care of Slava, we can really start fresh. I'll explain that he betrayed me, that he betrayed my mother. We're not to fuck with each other's families, and Slava and his goons know it. He was playing a dangerous game, and he knows he's lost."

"Once we take care of him," I correct.

He shakes his head.

"No, Sarah. It's been a mistake to let you get so far in. You can't get involved any more than you already are. That's my condition. When we get home, you leave my work to me, and you do your own thing."

"Dimitri, my own thing is spying! C'mon, you know I'm good at this. I can help you!"

"I can't let you get hurt, Sarah. Seeing you taken by those guys... By my own associates? How can you ask me to let you do that again?"

"But Dimitri—"

"No, Sarah. This is my one condition. If you can't handle this, then just walk away now. You have all the money you could ever want for, and I'd give you more. It doesn't mean anything to me if you're hurt or worse."

I pull back, looking at his face, trying to judge how serious he is, but I already know. He means it. I bite in on my lower lip, worrying it gently.

"But I can help you. I can keep you safe."

His fingers go into my hair as his forehead presses against mine.

"That's my job as a husband. Your job as a wife is to save me from what I have to do. Can you do that?"

Finally, I nod, because I finally understand what he needs me to be. He doesn't need me to be his spy or his lookout; he needs me to be his anchor. The spot of good that remains in his life and makes him feel better at the end of the day.

My mouth presses against his, tender and sweet, and his tongue traces along the seam of my lips.

"This will all be settled soon, lover," he growls as he rolls off of me, tugging me into his broad chest. "And then you can start planning our wedding."

CHAPTER 29

"Joanna?"

"Hey Sarah. I think I might have found something. This might be nothing. I looked into Slava and found little. I mean, the banks there are pretty shady, so nothing from that end. So then I started looking into Slava's family, but they never had anything there."

Inwardly I sigh.

"I get it, Joanna. I owe you more than a steak dinner for this favor."

"Hell yes you do. Anyways, long story short," she says sarcastically, "his father had taken a mistress, and she had a house in Cyprus. I figure if Slava's anywhere, he might be there."

I quickly take down the address, handing it to Dimitri. In seconds, he's out the door, and I'm left to worry.

* * *

AN HOUR PASSES, and there's no word from Dimitri. Nothing. Just silent, frustrating waiting. I think back on what he said, about how I need to be safe. That I need to provide him some stability.

It's not the girl I am, but it's the girl I could be, for him. If I don't need the money, after all, why should I put myself in danger?

I walk through the villa, trying to distract myself from my troubled thoughts.

Dimitri's going to be fine, I remind myself as I head towards the sauna. It's already hot as hell, but I could use the relaxation in my muscles. I strip out of my sundress until I'm fully nude, slipping into the warm, humid air.

It has a beautiful cedar scent to it, and I can't help but feel a little more at ease.

It clears my lungs, and I curl up onto the bench, a towel beneath my butt to keep me from burning myself.

Once Dimitri gets back, and Slava's taken care of, I'll be able to truly relax.

When I get out, I feel like the commercials always say: dewy. It makes the thick, Mediterranean air a bit easier to breath, and I start heading towards the bedroom when I hear a noise. I stop, gripping the towel about my breasts a bit tighter.

Silence.

It's all in your head, I chide myself. I'm just on edge, waiting for Dimitri. I take another few steps, but then I hear it again. Like nails on a chalkboard, but slightly quieter.

I grab my phone, speed dialing Dimitri.

What do I say? What if he doesn't pick up? I try to keep my pace slow and quiet, but all I want to do is run and hide under the covers. Dimitri's right. I'm not cut out for this feeling of fear.

Three rings and still he hasn't picked up.

Because he's dealing with Slava, I remind myself. There's no one here. It's all in my head.

Voicemail.

There is another sound behind me, on the far side of the villa. *Maybe it's just a stray cat.*

What if it isn't?

My inner mind is in turmoil, debating what to say on the phone. But if it is a person, if it is Slava, I need to let Dimitri know without tipping Slava off that I'm on to him.

"Hi Dimitri," I say, trying to sound natural. "I was just wondering if you've heard from our *uncle* yet. I think he might be coming over right now. I guess the wires got crossed? Anyways, when you get this, if you could come home, I'd really like that."

I hang up and glance behind me. No footsteps. No noises.

I didn't just screw Dimitri over because of an overactive imagination, did I? I move into the bedroom and lock the door behind me.

Quickly I throw on some pants and a t-shirt. It makes me feel a little less vulnerable to be clothed, and I take a moment to try to think.

What if it is Slava? I ask myself before I head to the drawers. Dimitri was able to smuggle a gun into the country, but it wasn't easy, and he definitely couldn't bring two. There isn't much in the room outside of our suitcases with a few pieces of clothing.

I start opening and closing drawers, looking for I'm not even sure what, and finding a big fat pile of nothing.

I go to the closet, standing on tiptoes as I grope along the top shelf when my hand finds something hard and wooden. I pull down a cricket bat, and test the grip in my hands.

Perfect.

With a momentary burst of confidence I head back into the living room towards where the sounds were coming from, but immediately something catches my notice.

The front door is open.

Not just a little.

It's wide open.

My heart skips a beat, and it's like time freezes.

It doesn't make any sense that it would be Dimitri having gotten back quickly; he'd have called out my name.

My hands grasp the bat tighter, and I edge towards the door, but all I see is the clear skies and greenery of the outside garden. If Slava's out there, he's hiding to either side of the door.

I can hear my own pulse in my ears as I move closer and closer to the door, until finally I reach out and grasp a hold of it and slam it shut. I want to lock it, but then a worry creeps through me.

What if he's already inside the house?

I clutch at the bat with both hands again and turn slowly around. I'm half expecting to see him right there behind me, waiting. But there's nothing. No one.

A battle rages in my own mind: do I try to hide in the manor? Or do I run outside and hope for the best?

The worst is that I'm paralyzed by not knowing. If he's already inside, running is the best option. If he's not? That'd be about the worst thing I could possibly do.

A creaking sound from the stairs makes me spin around and gasp, but there's nothing there that I can see.

Without realizing it I've been backing up in fright, and my shoulders bump against the wall as I seek some comfort. Knowing some direction is safe from approach. I edge closer towards the stairs, letting instinct drive me over reason, eschewing the front door.

As I reach the spiral staircase I peer up, to see if Slava had maybe made his way upstairs out of my view. But there's nothing there. I can't see any sign of him.

My nerves are so on edge that the sound of my own footsteps on the marble floor are making me cringe.

I debate going up the stairs, but decide against it. Instead I make my way towards the study, nestled just beyond the stairwell. It has a lock, I remember, and I tell myself I'll be safe there.

The door is shut, but once I'm there I slowly open it, peering behind me again at the calm, quiet manor before I shift my focus to the insides of the study.

Inside is the gaudy, multicultural layout of the room, with its Persian rugs, oriental vases, and paintings from around the world. But no sign of Slava. It looks safe. I breathe a sigh of relief, and for a second, I believe I've imagined it all.

A crack on the back of my head tells me I should've ran outside.

My vision blurs after the impact of the butt of the gun, and it's like I've lost time, but it can't be, because my attacker hasn't moved and I've not fallen over. It was a single rough blow to the back of my head, but it didn't do what my assailant hoped.

I scream out in a rage and on pure instinct and my limited training I strike with the bat, cracking into Slava's arm. I hit his wrist and he cries out, the gun flying from his hand and crashing to the floor in a noisy clatter before disappearing beneath an ottoman.

"Bitch!" he curses, but he only has the one arm available. The other is wrapped up, still hurt from the bullet wound Dimitri had given him.

I hit him again with the bat, still screaming my head off in my fright and worry. I make him back up as the blows hit him and I could cry I'm so glad I've not fucked it all up completely!

Slava puts an end to my hopes quickly though, grasping a hold of the bat in his one good arm and glowering at me. He's a strong, hardened man, and he won't be undone with some amateurish smacks of a cricket bat.

He curses at me in Russian and wrenches the bat from my grasp.

"You little bitch!" he says before hitting me with it, and my successful strikes all seemed so weak by comparison. A single blow from him and his one good arm and I crash against the wall and window.

The second blow is one I can't afford to take, and I roll out of the way just in time as he smashes out the expensive glass. A back-swipe catches me in the shoulder though and I sprawl to the floor.

My head is ringing, and I can't hear a thing he's saying as he strikes me in the back with the bat. He's a sadistic asshole, though, and once he's finished getting his petty revenge with it, he bends down, grasps me by the back of my shirt and lifts me off the floor before throwing me down again onto my back. He pins me down beneath his knees, his crushing weight making me cry out.

Slava's face is red with rage, such that if looks could kill I'd already be little more than dust or vapor.

"I am going to make your death a miserable fucking—"

I watch as Dimitri rushes in from outside. It's all like slow motion to me as the pain and anxiety boils in my blood. Dimitri pulls Slava off of me and my head falls back to the marble flooring. It's yet another hurt to add to the ones Slava has already given me, but I barely feel it this time.

Instead, I focus my awareness on trying to clear the blur from my vision. I watch as Dimitri pins Slava down beneath him, and his fists rain down blows.

From my position I can't see much. All I can see is Dimitri's upper body, the look of rage on his face that was more fearsome than Slava's ever was. And those two working arms of his don't stop.

I can't see Slava, but slowly I start to hear the world around me again, and the sickening sounds of fists impacting bone and flesh are filling the air. The cracks, the meaty thuds. Blood spatters into the air as Dimitri keeps going, his assault is unrelenting. Catching Slava atop me, hurting me, had let loose a caged animal that was starving. Starving for vengeance.

When at last I fainted, all I can remember is the gory sight of Dimitri, caked in blood and gore, and knowing that Slava must already be long dead.

* * *

A warm cloth on my forehead wakes me, Dimitri's bloodied face the first thing I see. It's not his blood, though. I know that. It's Slava's.

I glance to the side, a blanket draped over a body as his blood stains the expensive rug, pooling out beneath him. My heart begins racing again, and I look up at Dimitri with wide eyes.

"Shh," he coaxes, his words gentle. "He's gone. He can't hurt you anymore."

I'm not sure what it is that comes over me. Gratitude, maybe, or something far more primal than that. I lunge for Dimitri's mouth, and he stills, uncertain. Seconds pass, my arms wrapping around him, tugging him in closer.

He growls, animalistic, before he easily picks me

up off the floor and carries me into the next room. I'm helpless in his arms, my pain only numbed by my need to feel his body crushing mine. I need to feel alive, pain or no pain, and when he flings me to the couch and strips off his shirt, I know he feels the same way.

We're so grateful to be back in one another's arms, safe, and all that fear and worry oozes out of us into the thick need to screw.

Emotions are all connected in weird ways, or at least that's what I'm telling myself in my defense. But the panic of nearly being beaten to death, the horror of watching my lover snuff the life from my assailant, it flows from one to the other so well, then blends seamlessly into my need for Dimitri. A physical, carnal need.

My back is bruised and hurting, but that doesn't matter as he wraps his arms around me, holds me tight and kisses me deep. Those same powerful arms that had beaten a man into a bloody pulp now held me, and instead of mere revulsion, I felt comforted by it.

Through all my snooping and brazen prying, he had my back. Protected me. He went after the man who hurt me with more of a fiery vengeance that I could've imagined before now.

So I feel his hard body, hear the beat of his heart, and feel him tremble with rising need. His masculine rage turning to passion as quickly as my horror at his brutality turned to a need to screw.

My mouth goes down his jaw as my hands grab at his belt quickly undoing it. I am still sore, but more than that, I am aching to have him. To feel his hard, throbbing member against me. To thank him for protecting me.

Here we are, in this opulent manor, blood stained and messy as he hurriedly tugs off his belt, pulled open his trousers. That thick, throbbing shaft of his lies beneath the dark bulge in his boxer-briefs, and he yanks open my top. Those strong, hard hands grope at my chest, pulls my bra open, as I tug down his underwear and let that meaty shaft rise out, free and hard.

I hiss in a breath of pain as I push against him, and he looks concerned for a split second before my hand wraps around his cock, pumping it in my fist. I'm hurt, but more than anything else, I need this. Him. Carnally.

I tug him back to the floor, wanting more room to move and grind against him. It's messed up, but as he rolls to his back, I shimmy down his body, my mouth quickly wrapping around the head of his dick. It's my way of saying thank you, I guess. My way of letting him know how much I appreciate him saving my life.

Those are the selfless reasons.

The selfish ones are way too complicated for me to figure out right now.

His strong, stained hands go to my head, and he curls his fingers into my hair as my mouth goes down his shaft. His jaw juts out as he gives a low groan, tilting his head back as his cock swells with excitement.

The light scent of his masculine musk fills my nostrils as it wafts from his tuft of pubic hair. His thick girth bulging, its veiny mass stretching my mouth open wider, forcing my jaw back, proving himself to be more a mouthful than I was reckoning on.

He threatens my gag reflex, but I fight it. Thick saliva coats my mouth, lubricating his cock as my eyes water. It's so good, so perfect, and I stay there for a moment longer before pulling back, drawing air in through my nose.

It's only a second before I push back down again and feel him press against the back of my throat.

It's definitely the most poorly timed sexual escapade of my life, as short as the list is. But he's reclining back on one arm as the other holds my head, tangled into my hair at the back of my neck. His powerful arm helping guide me, urging me on as I do my best to shower my savior with affection.

His eyes are shut I notice when I flutter my long lashes and glance up at him. That chiseled face of his, those rugged good looks, marred by pleasures of the flesh, and a low, guttural groan escapes his lips.

My one hand goes to his abs, feeling along his muscles with appreciation as my other hand dips lower, between his thighs. I touch along his sack, my motions cautious and uncertain as my tongue wiggles along the underside of his cock.

In one hand I feel the hard, sculpted abs of his well-honed body, the other his one weak point. The one area on Dimitri that isn't guarded and tough. I roll those sensitive balls along my slender digits, tease them as he groans and moans. He's a caged lion as he rests beneath me, his body shifting, wanting to push me off and claim me, but he lets me have my fun. Lets me please him at my own pace, as torturous as that is.

His every husky moan a delightful encouragement, his every eager push at the back of my head a sign of how much he enjoys my mouth upon him and wants more.

I know it's all about his pleasure, and about making him happy, but at the same time... it's turning me on more than I could have imagined. He tastes sweet and a little salty, and every beat of his heart passes through him to throb against my tongue. It's intimate, and dirty, and I can't get enough.

I push myself down further, feel a slight ache at the back of my throat, and more thick saliva coats his member. I bounce off it for a second, looking up at him in his pleasured state. He's rendered docile by my mouth alone, and it makes me feel powerful as I push my lips back along his cock.

Slava couldn't beat him, the thugs who abducted me couldn't, but by the power of my warm mouth and moist tongue, I brought the mighty Dimitri to heel. He's a twitching, moaning mass of muscle beneath me, and I baste his cock with my tongue lashes, fondle his heavy, cum-laden balls with my soft, delicate fingers.

My hand pushes up along his stomach, and a stray glance at those chiseled abs let me soak in how glorious they look. A light sheen of perspiration from his savage rescue makes them gleam, and I can't help but rake my nails over them, make him squirm a little from the teasingly harsh contrasted to the delightfully soothing of my mouth.

To make a man like Dimitri moan so fully, it's such a buzz, a high like doing drugs, I imagine.

I moan, my body begins to grind against his wantonly. My legs straddle his calf, my bare chest rubbing across his thighs as I start losing myself more and more in the act. I barely know what I'm doing, nature having taken its course, but it's affecting me so quickly.

I remove my hand from his stomach, briefly bringing my fingers between my legs, petting myself for only a second over my pants.

Dimitri looks up at me, and as he watches me touch myself he seems to lose control.

In a swift, smooth motion, he rises up through the strength in his core muscles alone. He grabs a hold of my pants, yanks them open then tugs them down. He pushes me off of him, rolls me over onto my back on the floor, and frees me of panties along with my pants.

He's ravenous, and he lunges for my lips as he grasps my thighs in each hand, splaying my legs open wide as his saliva-glistening cock jabs at my slit. He's a wild animal, savage and lust filled. And I'm his next prey.

When he thrusts into me, though, it's like I've died and gone to heaven. I moan and arch my back, my body aching with need and the bruises of my beating.

I can still see the spatter of blood on his face and chest, the ruby stains on his hands. I saw how ruthlessly he dispatched Slava.

But it didn't repulse me. It didn't scare me away.

It just made me want him more. To know how dangerous, how ruthless he is, and to know that it's all been to protect me.

"Dimitri!" I cry out, my back rubbing against the marble flooring.

It's not lovey-dovey sex, it's not romantic love making, it's raw, hard fucking. It's brutal, it's savage, it's something that no civilized people should have the opportunity to experience any more in our day and age. But it's driving me wild!

Dimitri takes hold of my hips as he pounds into me, those powerful hands gripping my body as he makes me shake and scream, hammering that thick cock into me harder, harder. Moments before he was furiously pounding Slava's face in, now he's furiously rutting into me, and every pulse of his heart is a throb of his thick cock inside me, and I want it.

I want it all.

So maybe I'm a sinner just like him. Maybe I am damned or corrupted by his influence.

But I would throw away everything I have for him. I'd give everything up, would sacrifice it all, for this.

My head is foggy, my screams filling the villa, and the deeper he pounds into me, the more I yearn for him. I want him all. His kisses, his gentleness, and his brutality as well.

A shiver travels up and down my spine, and my whole body wriggles beneath him as I moan and cry out. Why? Not just the pleasure or pain of his hard, thrusting cock. Though that was enough to already make me squirm beneath him.

It was the sound. The wet sound of our flesh pounding together as he hammers between my thighs, thrusting his dick into my depths. That fleshy sound so eerily similar to the noises his fist made when he was brutally murdering a man in my defense.

The continuity of those sounds, of our depraved fucking, it all makes me heady with lust and I writhe almost away from him. But he reaches out, grasps my neck and holds me in place, forcing his lips to mine as he kisses me hard.

It scares me; it turns me on. My arms wrap around his neck, my nails digging into his flesh as I arch my back into him. Each thrust brings a spark of pain and pleasure, but this is about something more than just an orgasm.

This is about a connection. Acknowledging the very real truth about who we are to one another, and reveling in it. Our masks are cast aside, and even as his hand tightens around my throat just enough for me to really *feel* it, I know I've found the only man who could ever make me his.

How could I ever hope to find a man who would make me feel like this? Who could share such highs and lows of my life with? Fuck, I hope I never meet another man to go through these trying moments with!

Dimitri got me through, and the feeling of him inside me, filling me, making me so whole... it is bliss. And the awful, brutal events that led us here are nothing but fuel to our passions. My body shakes, my breasts rock and jiggle, and he grasps one, sinks his fingers into that fleshy mound as he pumps himself into me. Fucks me harder, faster, squeezes my neck tighter.

We've both lost our grip on reality, sanity blurring with the absolute craziness as his mouth presses against mine angrily. The passion between us is like fire, and it's consuming us both. We've thrown caution to the wind, and soared higher than I could ever have imagined.

My knees are bent up in the air as he pushes me down into the floor, my hips angled as he leans down into me. The loud slap of his balls against my ass resounding as he pummels me with that thick, throbbing cock. He bites my lower lip, and I bite him back.

I rake my nails over his chest, he squeezes my throat. I clench my pussy around his cock and he tugs my hair.

We're out of control, rutting like beasts as he grunts and groans, and I squeal and moan.

But inevitably we barrel towards our pleasured ends with one another. He's fast approaching his climax as he shudders above me.

Our bodies mash together, and I cling to him so tightly. His chest presses into mine, separated only by a thin film of sweat.

And now he finally hits that brink, his hand dips down, finding my clit, and he aggressively forces me over the edge as well. It takes so little, just the ruthless, almost angry touch of his rough finger against my throbbing, needful bud, and I lose all control.

My warm juices flood him, our bodies uniting in the most heavenly and sinful act imaginable.

While I spasm and squirm, writhing about in pleasure, he stiffens like a board, forcing me into place as he pumps me full of his seed. That hard body jackhammering a single, last thrust into my pussy as he unloads all his cum into my depths, making me quiver and shake. Making me the receptacle for all his passions. His virile spunk.

Until finally, finally, his powerful form gives way and he collapses atop me, resting on my body as we both pant and desperately try to catch our breaths.

I can feel that something vital has changed between us, something important.

And yet still, as he comes down from his explosive high, he turns loving, with gentle kisses and appreciative sounds. He's a savage thug, a ruthless mafia killer. But then in the after throes of our passionate rutting, he's tender again. And caring.

Always in those after moments, he's the kindest I've ever seen him. And I get to bask in the radiant warmth of his affections.

Though coming back down to reality leads to questions that may be dirtier than our sex. Like Slava's body in the other room.

* * *

Dimitri forces me into the bedroom for the rest of the night. He doesn't want me to see what he's about to do, and despite the passion of our love making, there's some things that even I don't want to have to know.

I'm exhausted as is, and for the first time since we arrived, I truly feel safe. Protected.

As I lay back on the bed, my eyes heavy, my body sore, I drift off, imagining our wedding.

CHAPTER 30

My feet ache from running all around the city, getting our wedding photos done, but honestly, I'm so excited to get them developed. The ceremony was amazing, if a little over the top, but I'm most excited for the toasts. Since Dimitri and I are now parentless, he promised me something special.

Music plays as the crowd arrives to the restaurant, the lights dim and give off a pale, purple glow. I still can't believe we're finally married, and my hands run self-consciously over the baby bump that's just starting to show beneath my wedding gown.

"You look great," Dimitri says for the tenth time today, his hand drawing mine away as he leans in and kisses my cheek. "Don't fret about it, my wife."

I'm still not used to hearing him say that, and it sends a shiver of excitement through me.

More and more people enter the room, finding their seating, and then the room goes silent. An old man, probably in his sixties, enters along with a woman draped in pearls and fur. Even Dimitri quiets down, sitting a bit taller, and so I follow suit.

When the man goes to the podium and I see the twinkle in Dimitri's eye, I know this is important to him.

"My friends, colleagues. Strangers." The crowd laughs politely, even Joanna. She must sense something about him too.

"For those who don't know me, I'm Aleksey Dmitriev, and I absolutely warned Dimitri against this wedding."

My heart stops, until Aleksey looks right at me and smiles.

"That was before I knew what type of woman Sarah Fairfax really is. The courage, the fire within her, reminds me of my own beautiful wife, Inga. When Dimitri asked me for my blessing, I refused. When he asked again, I knew he was serious. I still refused. But when he told me that she's truly the one, and explained why... I gave my blessing without him asking. So this is to the happy couple. May they forever find themselves in the embrace of family."

He looks back at the crowd, and Dimitri squeezes my hand.

Two servers come up, pouring up a shot glass of Russian vodka for him, and water for me. We clink glasses and take the shot, but as soon as I swallow the crowd erupts in chants.

"Gorko! Gorko!"

I look at Dimitri and he grabs my jaw, bringing my mouth to his before invading my lips with his tongue. The entire restaurant cries out with joy and their clapping sounds like an earthquake. When Dimitri finally breaks the kiss, the taste of vodka is gone with him.

Aleksey smiles, and raises his own shot glass before downing his vodka, returning to his toast.

"I knew Dimitri's father well. We came up together. I respected him, but I do not give respect freely. Rebecca, Dimitri's mother, was cunning. Clever. When she was killed by that snake, Slava, he crossed us. He forgot what family meant to me. To us! But Dimitri and Sarah know, better than most, what family means." There's a hidden joke there, and I can't help but flush at the reminder.

"To the lovely bride, and the handsome groom. To their lost parents, and their found family."

The crowd claps again, and Dimitri kisses against my ear as the band takes the stage. He grabs my hand, dragging me upwards and towards the dance floor.

"Our first dance as husband and wife," I say with a glee I couldn't have anticipated, and he's just as thrilled. The song is one we picked out together, a beautiful, voiceless piece of classical music that reverberates through our bones.

My arms wrap around his neck, his arms around my waist, and all eyes are on us as we dance.

"This is amazing, Dimitri."

His mouth presses against my forehead.

"It's no less than you deserve."

"So that's your... boss?"

"*Da*."

I know better than to pry into that statement, so instead I rest my head against his chest. Things are right between Dimitri and his *bratva*. His brotherhood. He told me that Slava had been raising a lot of eyebrows as he started taking more and more matters into his own hands, cutting out the *bratva* of their share of profits. But when they found that he was the one that killed Rebecca, all bets were off. You don't do that to protected people or their loved ones.

And Dimitri and I? We're now protected. Safe.

A pile of envelopes has gathered on the gift table, along with several large and beautifully wrapped presents that I can't wait to open. Music plays all around us, dancing bodies moving onto the dance floor, and the entire evening is spent in joy and bliss.

This is my life now. A double edged sword of passion and fear, of pain and pleasure.

Dimitri's finger brings my chin upwards, his

mouth pressing aggressively against mine before his breath washes over my ears with a promise. A threat.

"Tonight, I'm going to really make you scream *uncle*, and mean it."

I can't wait to see how.

* * *

THANK you so much for reading! I hope you enjoyed <3 If you have a moment, please leave a review. Other readers are dying to know what you thought.

I have plenty more bad boy romance for you, so make sure you check out my other books on the next couple of pages, and sign up for my newsletter to be notified when I have a new release on the way!

~Alexis Abbott

Killing For Her

Abducted

Stepbrothers:

Ruthless

Criminal

Standalones:

Betting on Love

Hunter's Baby

I Hired A Hitman

Vegas Boss

Rock Hard Bodyguard

Innocence For Sale: Jane

Redeeming Viktor

Romance:

Falling for her Boss (Novella)

Most Wanted: Lilly (Novella)

Bound as the World Burns (SFF)

Erotic Thriller:

The Dangerous Men Series:

The Narrow Path

Strayed from the Path

Path to Ruin

ABOUT THE AUTHOR

Alexis Abbott is a Wall Street Journal & USA Today bestselling author who writes about bad boys protecting their girls! Pick up her books today if you can't resist a bad boy who is a good man, and find yourself transported with super steamy sex, gritty suspense, and lots of romance.

She lives in beautiful St. John's, NL, Canada with her amazing husband.

facebook.com/abbottauthor

twitter.com/abbottauthor

instagram.com/alexisabbottauthor

bookbub.com/authors/alexis-abbott

pinterest.com/badboyromance

youtube.com/AlexisAbbott

ACKNOWLEDGMENTS

Thank you to my amazing Patrons. I'm constantly humbled and grateful for your support.

Ramona Cabrera
Melissa Hedrick
Virginia Swanson
Dawn Daughenbaugh
Don Doss
Stacie Currie

If you'd like to join them — and get my ebooks or paperbacks — you can find me here on Patreon.
https://www.patreon.com/alexisabbott

www.ingramcontent.com/pod-product-compliance
Lightning Source LLC
Chambersburg PA
CBHW061609190726

48288CB00007B/2246